"Do you want to move?"

"Oh, *nee*, we don't need to move." The beginnings of a smile touched Rachel's face and her cheeks pinkened. "I think the crying has something to do with the *boppeli*." She wrinkled her nose. "But, regarding the fear, I…I don't think I'm ready to confront it yet. I still feel a bit foolish about it."

Ben's heart rate sputtered. "You shouldn't. We all have fears. Everyone is afraid of something. Even me."

Rachel rolled her eyes. "I can't believe that. You? Mr. Hero? Who jumped into a frozen pond to rescue an *Englisch* boy who fell through the ice?"

Ben's lips twitched into a half grin. "I didn't have enough time to think of being afraid then."

Rachel's dark brown eyes teasingly narrowed under her delicate brows. "When you have time to think, what are you afraid of?"

His smile evaporated. "Depends on the hour," he joked.

But he took a step back.

His greatest fear was never far from his mind.

I'm afraid you'll never love me like you love my brother…

Growing up on a farm, **Jocelyn McClay** enjoyed livestock and pursued a degree in agriculture. She met her husband while weight lifting in a small town—he "spotted" her. After thirty years in business management, they moved to an acreage in southeastern Missouri to be closer to family when their eldest of three daughters made them grandparents. When not writing, she keeps busy hiking, bike riding, gardening, knitting and substitute teaching.

Books by Jocelyn McClay

Love Inspired

The Amish Bachelor's Choice
Amish Reckoning
Her Forbidden Amish Love
Their Surprise Amish Marriage

Visit the Author Profile page at Harlequin.com.

Their Surprise
Amish Marriage

Jocelyn McClay

LOVE INSPIRED
INSPIRATIONAL ROMANCE

LOVE INSPIRED®
INSPIRATIONAL ROMANCE

ISBN-13: 978-1-335-75862-0

Their Surprise Amish Marriage

Love Inspired
22 Adelaide St. West, 40th Floor
Toronto, Ontario M5H 4E3, Canada
www.Harlequin.com

Printed in U.S.A.

As far as the east is from the west, so far
hath he removed our transgressions from us.
—*Psalm* 103:12

Always, I thank God for this opportunity.

Kevin, there could never be a more amazing service-oriented hero. I'm glad you're mine.

Thanks to Dad, I was raised around cattle, although they were beef, not dairy.

Thanks to two dairy-farming uncles who let me trail after them at milking time.

Brother-in-law Craig, thanks for sharing your experience with broken ribs.

Audra, I watched you handle a twin pregnancy with much mental, if not physical, grace. I watch you display the same grace as you parent my grandchildren, twins Eli and Amelia and older brother Judah, who bring me much joy.

Chapter One

She had to tell him. Stealing a glance at the dark-haired man across the grove, Rachel Mast rested her hand against her stomach. She didn't know if this bout of nausea was exacerbated by the thought of telling Benjamin, or just another round in the seemingly endless succession she'd had lately. In this case, it was most likely just the thought of talking to Ben. They hadn't exchanged a word with each other since the day Aaron left. Since the day they'd… Swallowing against the prickling sensation at the back of her throat, Rachel pressed her hand more tightly against her stomach. She had to tell him.

Mired in thought, she flinched when words were spoken just off her shoulder.

"I'm so glad Ben came today. His appearances at these events have been about as rare as yours." Rebecca's comments told Rachel her younger sister's attention was also on the man chatting with a young Amish woman while he tapped a spile into a maple several trees away.

Turning her back on the couple, Rachel took the

clean pail from Rebecca to hang its handle on the hook tacked via a spile to their tree. "We were both baptized into the church this fall. Maybe we've felt ending our *rumspringa* meant no longer attending the *youngie* gatherings." Or maybe Ben felt the same guilt and shame she did. In the past six weeks, it'd been a race to see who'd depart a room the fastest when the other one appeared.

"But neither of you are married."

Rachel felt the blood drain from her face. Rebecca's mittened hand flew to her mouth. "I mean… I know you thought you'd be married to Aaron by now. I'm… I'm sorry I mentioned…" Reaching out, she touched Rachel's shoulder before turning to hurry back to the sled, parked in the middle of the grove behind two winter-coated Belgian horses. Rachel knew Rebecca's haste was more an embarrassed escape rather than a need to gather additional pails for the clusters of young people tapping the nearby maple trees for syrup.

Upon reaching the sled, Rebecca anxiously glanced in her direction. Rachel sighed. She couldn't blame her sister. Rachel had been counting down the days until her and Aaron's wedding announcement could be made. All plans were in place for a customary late fall wedding. Until Aaron had been kicked by a horse on baptism Sunday, spending the morning at the hospital getting a complicated fracture set instead of becoming a member of the church along with Rachel.

Although sorely disappointed, Rachel hadn't despaired. Aaron would surely be baptized sometime after the Christmas season so they could be married. No one, least of all her, expected him to disappear into the *Englisch* world in January, a few days prior to doing so. And she couldn't follow him—even if she knew where he went—as having been baptized, she'd be shunned if she left.

Inconsolable, Ben—also stunned by his brother's departure—had given her a ride home so they could commiserate in private. Rachel flushed as she recalled the shock and grief that had extended to comfort being sought. And offered. Which had led to...

Sagging against the tree, Rachel warmed chilled hands on her now-heated cheeks as she watched the clear liquid spilling down the spile into the bucket, an indication the maple sap was indeed running. She wished everything were just as clear to her. How naive she'd been, when her life had seemed so simple a few months ago. *Oh, Aaron, why did you leave? When are you coming back? Are you coming back?*

If Ben had heard from Aaron, surely he'd have told someone who would've mentioned it to her?

Rachel pressed her fingers against her throbbing temples. Even though the late February afternoon was just above freezing, she began to perspire. "Be sure your sin will find you out." *Ach*, the Old Testament verse was certainly true in this case. Rachel swallowed against another bout of nausea. Being sick in the snow would only raise questions she couldn't answer. And she had enough of those herself. What would Ben say? Would he believe her? Would he ask her to marry him? What if he didn't? What if she wed Ben and Aaron came back? Marriage was for life. Her nose prickled with the threat of tears. There seemed no good options.

What if she waited, and didn't marry, leaving her to face even more shame? And Aaron never returned? Pressing her cheek against the rough bark of the maple tree, Rachel panted shallowly, the crisp winter air a contrast to the bile at the back of her throat.

She was running out of time. She had to tell Benjamin.

Benjamin Raber gently tapped the spile into the maple tree, listening—without hearing—to the constant chatter from the woman at his elbow. He was glad Lydia Troyer had clung to him like a cocklebur to a horse's mane upon his arrival at the *youngies* outing. It kept him from talking with others. It helped keep his eyes from straying, like they did now to the tall brunette woman across the way, currently resting her head with its neatly pinned *kapp* against a tree.

Frowning, Ben stilled his hands as his eyes narrowed. Was Rachel all right? He shifted his weight in her direction before, tightening his lips, Ben continued with his task. Rachel didn't need his help. Not that she'd tell him either way. She was like a startled deer whenever she came in sight of him now, the way she'd jump and dash off. Besides, he wouldn't know what to say to her anyway. Lead congregated in his stomach. Or what he'd say to his brother if he ever saw him again.

"Are you all right?"

He blinked at Lydia's question, having momentarily forgotten she was there.

"*Ja.*" Ben redirected his hammer, glad he'd been tapping gently instead of swinging away when he hit his hand. Of course, a whack to the head might be just what he needed. Firming his jaw, he took the bucket from Lydia and set it on the hook. A whack to the head was surely what he'd needed weeks ago when a teary-eyed Rachel had curled against his chest and whispered, *I'm so glad you're here with me. Could you just hold me?* Ben stared unseeing at the silver lid as he fastened it to the top of the spile. Of course he had. He'd dreamed of holding Rachel for years. When she'd looked up at him, it'd seemed the most natural thing in the world to kiss her. And when she'd kissed him back...

"Wait up!" He could hear Lydia crunching through the snow behind him as he stalked to the next tree. "I thought you said that tree was big enough to support another tap and bucket."

Ben grunted. "Sometimes just because something is possible, it doesn't mean you should do it. It leads to... trouble." Plucking the drill from where he hooked it on his belt, Ben placed it against the bark, angled up so when the sap flowed, it would drip down to the bucket.

Lydia placed her mittened hand over Ben's bare fingers. Furrowing his brow, he looked up to see her simpering smile at a very, very close distance.

"I hope you don't really feel that way. Because I'm hoping it's possible you give me a ride home today."

Ben's fingers flexed and the sound of the power drill cut into the crisp afternoon. Lydia jerked her hand and herself back. Thankful to have borrowed the drill from the furniture shop where he worked, Ben shifted his attention back to the tool in his hand. He sighed as he continued his task. He wished he had the glib tongue of his friend and former coworker, Samuel Schrock. Samuel would know how to flirt back. Or did before he was married. Ben's brother, Aaron, also would've known how to respond. Only too well. Ben's hands tightened. He winced when the drill bit cut farther into the maple than he'd intended. Carefully withdrawing it, he patted the tree, silently apologizing.

Clearing wood shavings from the edge of the newly drilled hole, he gave Lydia what he hoped passed as a smile. "I need to get back home. Got to help with chores tonight."

He didn't have to; it was the quickest excuse he could think of. But, having said it, it's what he would do. That was the way Ben worked. His folks would surely be surprised to see him home early today, as he was only here this afternoon because his mother had basically kicked him out of the house. *Things need to go back to some semblance of normal around here. We don't know why Aaron left, when or even if he's coming back.* She'd pinned Benjamin with a look. *I'm tired of you pacing around the house like a lonely goat when you're not at work. Aaron is gone. That doesn't change our lives. We have to go on.*

Ben's younger siblings were attending the event, an activity planned when the late February weather finally warmed up enough during the day to prompt the sap to run. Ben had wanted to come, while simultaneously wanting to avoid it. The reason for his conflict was leaning against a tree several yards distant.

Except that she wasn't. Not anymore. A stolen glance revealed Rachel had straightened and was staring in his direction. Ben fumbled the spile and hook he was pulling from his pocket, almost dropping them into the snow. This was the first time she'd looked at him in weeks. Surprisingly, she held his gaze. He felt as frozen as the snowman some of the younger attendants had rolled up in the small clearing.

Was she as embarrassed and ashamed as he was?

Was she all right? Her face was almost as white as the snow layered on the branch of the tree above her head.

"Are you ready for this yet?"

Reluctantly, Ben turned to see Lydia holding up the bucket she carried. His gaze dropped to the recently bored hole. The one that held no hook or spile. The one obviously not ready for a pail. The only thing obviously ready was this woman for his attention. Lifting his eyes again to Lydia, he saw her gaze shift from his face to somewhere over his shoulder. In the direction where Rachel stood.

"I wonder what Rachel is going to do now that Aaron left. I mean, everyone knew they were going to get married. The Masts' garden was full of celery this summer, planning for a wedding. I heard she even had her blue dress made. If I were her, I'd feel rejected. No wonder she was crying her eyes out that day."

Ben carefully set the spile, with the hook behind it, at the edge of the new hole, his teeth gritted. Rigidly controlling his actions, he gently tapped it in. The one he wanted to reject was Lydia. But it wasn't her fault. She'd just stated the obvious. He knew the pain Rachel had felt. Was surely still feeling. Pain he wanted to take away. His stomach soured at the knowledge that he'd made it worse by his actions in trying to do so.

"Ready for the pail."

After Lydia hooked the bucket under the spile, Ben attached the lid that would keep precipitation or other debris out of the pail. A quick glance over his shoulder showed Rachel was still looking in his direction. Inhaling deeply, Benjamin warmed up his smile and turned to try it on Lydia.

He injected fabricated enthusiasm into his voice.

"Looks like we'll need some more buckets. And I could certainly use a cup of the hot chocolate if they still have it."

The red-haired young woman's immediate return smile dipped to a frown when she saw the congregation surrounding the sled and the thermoses brought along for the outing. "Be right back."

"Take your time," Ben called as she tromped through the snow to join the growing line. After another considering look at Rachel, he started walking through the trees, away from the crowd, and at an angle that would converge with her. Should she decide to take a stroll. A sideways glance revealed she had. Ben's heart rate accelerated. It was a struggle to prevent his pace from doing so, as well.

Their paths intersected about thirty yards deeper into the trees. Here, oaks interspersed with the maples, creating a denser wood, and therefore a less attractive destination to any potential tappers. The snow was shallower. Ten pristine feet of it separated him from Rachel when they both slowed to a stop.

It was the closest he'd been to her in almost two months. This girl, who unknowingly had been his secret childhood longing until she became his brother's girlfriend. Their relationship, although stilted, had remained cordial. It'd had to. She was going to be his sister-in-law. Even though it tormented Ben to see her with his brother. And now they were…awkward. Uncomfortable. Embarrassed. *Ach*, had they sabotaged their friendship beyond any salvaging?

Frowning, Ben silently regarded Rachel. Framed by her pale face, her brown eyes, normally so lively, seemed bigger and darker above hollow-appearing cheeks. Her arms were crossed over her torso. If she hugged herself any tighter, she'd turn inside out.

"Are you cold?" Ben crossed his own arms to keep from reaching out to comfort her. If she were looking for something like that, she wouldn't have stopped ten feet away. Not that he would offer it again. Succumbing to the urge to give comfort had gotten them to this unhappy place.

Rachel slid her arms down to her sides. *"Nee."*

They stared at each other across the snow for a few more moments.

Ach, it'd been quite a long wait for those few important words. Ben grimaced and shifted his weight. There was so much he wanted to say to her. But where to start? Perhaps with the obvious, but not the one particular obvious he wanted to ask—are you all right after what we did? Perhaps he could leave it at *are you all right?* But even that currently sounded too personal.

He settled for something that was surely on both their minds, "Have you heard from—" stopping when he heard her ask the same question.

Her *nee* was a softer echo of her previous one. He shook his head at her hopeful gaze.

Refolding her arms across her chest, Rachel looked down to where she was making semicircles with one foot in the snow in front of her. "Benjamin…"

Ben crept a few steps closer in order to hear, her voice had dropped so low.

"About that day…"

He flushed with embarrassment. What about that day? Could they get past their shame and bear to be in the same room with each other once more? Had she decided she never wanted to see him again? That seemed more consistent with her actions the past several weeks. Ben braced himself for her next words. Whatever they might be, he would abide by them out of respect for her. He could see from Rachel's expression that the unspoken words were difficult to share.

Previously perspiring, now a chill prompted him to flip up the collar of his coat. Still, Rachel's words were nothing like he'd expected.

"I'm going to have a *boppeli*."

Chapter Two

The blood drained from Ben's face at a pace likely exceeding all the sap running from the recently tapped maples. Stumbling to a nearby oak, he braced an arm against the furrowed bark of its trunk. Of all the things he'd thought of that night, and he'd thought a lot, he hadn't considered this. But he should have. He lived on a farm where managing livestock supported their livelihood.

Lifting his head, he stared at Rachel, whose white face was surely a reflection of his. "You're sure?"

Avoiding his gaze, she bobbed her head once. *"Ja."* The whisper drifted to him across the feet separating them.

Inhaling sharply, Ben straightened from the tree. He stepped toward Rachel, only to halt abruptly at a call from behind him.

"There you are! Here's your hot chocolate. Although hot probably won't describe it any longer."

Ben pivoted to see Lydia descending upon them, a smile on her lips while her hooded eyes shifted rapidly between him and Rachel. The hand he'd been extending toward Rachel reluctantly moved to accept the unwanted cup of chocolate. Not knowing what else to do, Ben concentrated on keeping his tremors under control so the dark brown contents didn't splatter over the snow as he carefully brought the cup to his lips and took a sip.

"Denki," he choked out as some of the lukewarm liquid went down the wrong tube in his tight throat. Thanks was not what he wanted to tell Lydia. Ben's gaze swept over the woman he longed to talk with— *needed* to talk with—then returned to the one he needed to sidetrack from her. Stepping between the two females, he reluctantly gave his physical attention to the one, while his awareness and emotions were fixed on the other.

The sound of Rachel's deep sigh reverberated through him. It was followed a moment later by the crunch of the snow as she walked away. It took all his willpower not to look in her direction as he headed back toward the gathering by the sled, Lydia walking close enough beside him for her arm to brush his elbow. Her dangling hand bumped against his own. Shifting the cup to that hand, Ben lifted it out of range.

"Thanks again for the chocolate. It's just what I needed before the drive home."

"Are you sure you don't want company?"

Ach, he surely did. Just not hers. "I'm *gut*. Got a few more things to take care of this evening than I expected." Like dealing with the concept of becoming a father. Ben stumbled at the realization, the hot chocolate arcing out in front of them to drop like a dark rain onto the snow.

To his chagrin, Lydia used the excuse to latch on to his arm. "Are you all right?"

Nee. He was far from all right. He'd betrayed his brother. He'd put himself and a friend he'd always cared for—*even loved?*—in a precarious situation. Ben's feet continued to move of their own accord while the arm Lydia hung from was as stiff as the oak tree he'd recently leaned against.

Rachel was going to have a baby. Ben's heart began to race. *They needed to get married.* His heart rate picked up even faster. Marrying Rachel had been his dream for years. The breathless smile that lifted the corners of his mouth froze. *But what about when Aaron comes back?* Ben had reluctantly watched the relationship between his brother and the girl he loved develop from the time she'd started her *rumspringa* at sixteen. Aaron Raber and Rachel Mast. Amish courtships were usually kept secret but the knowledge of those two together was so ingrained in their Plain community in the past four years, it was like saying salt and pepper.

What if Rachel wouldn't marry him? What if Aaron came back to wed Rachel and he had to watch his brother raise his child? Ben's steps slowed. The plastic cup crumpled in his suddenly tightened fist, the remainder of the cold chocolate dribbled from his hand. At his shoulder, Lydia glanced at him with a furrowed brow.

Ben shook his head, warding off her questions. "*Ach*, just a lot of things to do tonight. Much more than I expected," he murmured. Much, much more.

Lydia nodded, patting his coat-covered arm with one of her hands that encircled it. "I suppose Aaron's departure has prompted some changes."

Ben's breath whistled out through clenched teeth. He couldn't agree more.

Even though the temperature had dropped with the setting sun, firmly lodging itself below freezing, Ben's gloveless hands were sweating. He wiped them down the sides of his pants as he walked up the sidewalk to the Masts' front porch.

He'd known Susannah Mast for years. He'd always respected Rachel's *mamm*. She'd witnessed and laughingly forgiven him for many youthful transgressions when he'd played as a youngster in a group with her daughters. Ben's ears burned. She wouldn't be laughing about this one. Swallowing hard, he mounted the stairs and crossed the porch. He took another deep breath before he could rap his knuckles on the door.

The dim glow of an interior lamp shone through a window, advising folks were home. Still, Ben flinched, conscious of the last words they'd spoken, when the door opened to reveal Rachel. The solemn expression on her lovely face told Ben he'd been expected. But was his presence welcomed? He'd soon find out.

Thoughts of how to handle the unsettling situation had overwhelmed Ben as he helped his father—who was surprised with his unexpected appearance—with chores. As he'd flung bales of hay to the cattle, Ben had practiced proposing to them. None had accepted. He was afraid he'd get the same response from Rachel.

But he had to try. Marrying her had been his dream. But not like this. Not in a situation that was surely a nightmare to her.

Rachel stepped back, opening the door farther to allow him entrance. Ben swept off his knitted winter cap, wondering if he should've worn his black felt hat for the occasion. What was the proper protocol for proposing to his brother's girlfriend? Ben stifled a snort. There surely wasn't anything related to the topic in the district's *Ordnung.* He bit the inside of his cheek at the thought of the community's set of rules they'd obviously disobeyed. A confession—perhaps, even probably a public one—was required of both of them. Ben's stomach churned at the thought.

Susannah looked up from where she stood at the sink washing milking gear and smiled. Along with keeping bees, the Masts milked some goats that Susannah and her family used to make soaps and other items to sell.

"Ben, how nice to see you. Do you think we'll have a good year of sugaring? I asked Rachel, but she hasn't said much about the day."

"*Ja.* Sap seems to be running pretty *gut.*"

Susannah shook water from her hands and reached for a dish towel. "What brings you over this evening?"

Ben wadded the knit cap in his fist. "I… I was wondering if Rachel would like to go for a drive."

Raising an eyebrow, Susannah looked from him to her silent daughter and back again.

"I'll grab a blanket and my cloak."

Ben's tense shoulders dipped in relief at Rachel's words. He couldn't tear his eyes from her as she hastened to collect the items from the room. She was with child. Did she look different? His gaze lingered on her face. There was no evidence of the animation that normally lit her eyes. Her eyes looked tired. She looked tired.

He was aware that under her furrowed brow, Susannah's thoughtful gaze followed them out the door.

"Does she know?" Ben's voice was quiet as he trailed Rachel down the porch steps.

"Nee." Her words and a waft of condensation drifted over her shoulder. "No one knows but you."

Ben sighed as he watched her black-cloaked figure precede him through the yard's gate. Folks might not know now, but with Rachel's slender form, it wouldn't be long before they would. He stopped to free his mare, Sojourner, from the hitching post. Ben's tongue felt as tied as the knot he fumbled with. He wasn't good with words. Would he find enough appropriate ones to convince Rachel to marry him?

The prospect wasn't looking good when he climbed into the buggy to see Rachel sitting so far on the opposite side she was in danger of falling off the seat. The blanket she'd brought was piled between them like an instant mountain. Backing his horse away from the post, Ben studied his passenger's profile. He didn't speak until they pulled out of the lane and onto the country road. His pounding heart greatly exceeded the steady clip-clop of Sojy's slow jog.

"Denki for coming out. And for…telling me."

Her soft sigh carried to him on the quiet night. "I had to. Much better sooner than later."

"No word from…?"

Rachel shook her head before her chin dipped to rest against her chest.

Ben's fingers flexed on the leather reins. "I know I'm not the one you wanted, but, since you're having a *boppeli*… I'll marry you." He cringed as he heard the words fall out of his mouth. He'd done better proposing to the cattle. Another deep sigh from Rachel. Ben counted sixty-seven beats of Sojourner's hooves before she spoke.

"I'd like to make our confession to John Stoltzfus."

At least it wasn't an outright *no* to his question. It was a better outcome than he might have hoped, given the way he'd bungled it.

"Sounds *gut*. When?"

"If it's all right with you, I'd like to get it over with."

Ben nodded. When they reached the intersection, he turned the mare in the direction of the Stoltzfus dairy farm. "How are you feeling?"

Rachel turned to him with a weak half smile. "I've been better."

What did that mean? Had she been sick? Years ago, Ben might have coaxed her to expand upon her short answer. But that was before she and Aaron became a couple. When their relationship became apparent while other Amish courtships were usually kept under wraps, Ben's comments when he was with them had dwindled. The pair seemed to have so much to say to each other that, when they were all together, his contributions to the conversation weren't needed. Even the evening after Aaron's disappearance, he hadn't said much. He'd just wanted to be there to offer Rachel support. But while he may not have said much, he'd unfortunately done plenty. Ben's head sunk lower as he hunched his shoulders. Apparently, the less he said and did the better.

Twenty minutes later, and with fewer words than that spoken between them, he turned Sojourner into the Stoltzfuses' lane. Upon drawing to a stop, Ben descended and hurried around the buggy to assist Rachel down. How much help did a woman six weeks with child require anyway? He didn't recall any of the times his *mamm* had been with child. He had younger siblings, but he'd been pretty young as well when they were born. If the Amish kept courtships under wraps, they definitely didn't speak of pregnancies. Ben flushed at his ignorance. Things would seem normal, then there'd be some excitement and female company, and the next day there'd be a *boppeli*. He didn't know anything about being a husband to a woman with child. That knowledge, or lack of, had him breaking a sweat.

By the time he reached Rachel's side of the buggy, she was on the ground, twisting her hands together. "Do you think they'll put us under the *Bann*?"

"I don't know. In past situations, if they have, it hasn't been for long. We might be out for a Sunday or two."

At Rachel's anxious expression, Ben hastened to assure her, "I think you made a wise suggestion in choosing to confess to John Stoltzfus. I'd rather face him than Bishop Weaver or another minister."

"He was a friend of my *daed*'s. I thought he might be more…sympathetic." She grimaced. "But he might be more disappointed, as well."

Ben winced. The minister would be one of many in the community. "Well, we're here now."

Glancing about the surrounding farmyard in the early dusk of the February day, Ben's attention sharpened on the dim glow visible through the windows of the large barn. With his help, their farm's chores had been early, but the Rabers didn't have as many cows as the Stoltzfuses did. "Looks like he might be in the barn. I don't know what time he normally milks. Shall we go see?"

When he returned his gaze to Rachel, Ben bit his lip at the forlorn figure she made. Knowing how he felt, and that she felt the same or worse, he strove to provide whatever support he could, extending a hand toward her. Glancing at it, Rachel frowned before looking toward the barn and crossing her arms. With a deep sigh, Ben let his hand drop.

Rachel longed to take Ben's hand. But not if it would lead her into the barn. On top of being anxious and physically miserable, she felt so stupid. What kind of Amish girl was afraid of cows?

Ach, this one was. When she was a little girl, she'd been so excited to see a newborn calf she'd rushed into the pen and gotten too close to the new mama and her baby. The protective cow had knocked Rachel down, stepping on her several times in the process. Rachel had been terrified of cattle ever since, particularly Holsteins, one of the larger of the dairy breeds. Fortunately for her, unrelated to her harrowing adventure, her folks had traded out the cow for some goats shortly afterward. She hadn't been around cattle since, which was more than fine with her.

"Hello?" The call came from the house, where Mrs. Stoltzfus had stepped onto the porch to investigate the new arrival.

Returning her wave, Ben quietly asked, "Do you want to wait in the house?"

Rachel gave him a heartfelt smile. *"Ja. Denki."* The weight of his gaze followed her as she made her way across the ruts of the yard, where slush was refreezing after the warmth of the day. Mary Stoltzfus ushered her inside. The minister's wife obviously had other folks drop in to see her husband and thankfully didn't ask any questions. She and Rachel chatted about community events until the door opened and the men stepped inside. Although Ben met her gaze with an encouraging smile, any ease Rachel had developed with Mary's comfortable conversation evaporated at their arrival.

After getting her husband a cup of tea, Mrs. Stoltzfus made herself scarce. Rachel tipped up one side of her mouth at the unmistakable scent of cows wafting from the older dairyman. The odor didn't bother her at all. It was just the animal itself that scared her witless.

Settling into his chair, John Stoltzfus wore a smile on the weathered face above his graying beard. "Benjamin said you wanted to speak with me?"

Rachel had always liked her *daed*'s friend. The two had been ministers together in the district, up until Vernon Mast passed away. From John Stoltzfus's curious expression, he wasn't sure why they were there, but looked hopeful that it was for some positive occasion.

Unfortunately, that wasn't the case, although she supposed weddings in the Amish community were always considered a positive event. But was she going to marry Ben? Rachel hugged her arms to her chest. She hadn't answered him, and in his Ben-like manner, he hadn't pushed her. This wasn't his fault. She'd felt jilted, abandoned, deserted when his brother had left. Aaron had become so much of her identity. What was she without him? The night he'd left, she'd reached out for comfort, some type of affirmation, and Ben had provided it. He was a *gut* man and didn't deserve this situation.

Still, she didn't know how to answer her *daed*'s old friend. Clearing her throat, Rachel sent a beseeching glance to where Ben sat motionless in a nearby rocker. She saw his hands tightened on the ends of the chair's wooden armrests before he shifted and straightened in the seat.

"Um…*ja*. We need to make a…confession."

"A confession?" Mr. Stoltzfus frowned. Brow furrowed, he considered them both, his gaze darted back and forth between her and Ben before his face drooped into sorrowful lines. "*Ach*. I'm sorry to hear of the need. Best tell me though."

Haltingly, she and Ben separately confessed to their sins, Rachel reddening as much during Ben's confession as she had during her own. To her surprise, Ben was adamant that he was the instigator of the regretful situation. She slid a glance at him from below lowered eyelids, knowing it wasn't true. Still, she appreciated his actions. That was Ben, always stepping up to take care of things.

"And do you repent? Are you sorry for your sins and seek forgiveness?"

"Most assuredly." Their fervent responses were in unison.

"That's *gut*. And now, are you getting married?" The minister pinned Ben with a gaze as pointed as the tines of a pitchfork.

"I…uh…" Rachel saw Ben's throat bob as he swallowed. "I've asked. That will be Rachel's decision."

"And are you getting married?" Now John Stoltzfus's intent yet sympathetic eyes focused on Rachel. It was the sympathy from her *daed*'s friend that did her in. That and the hopeful look on Ben's face before he quickly controlled his expression. He was the father of the child she carried. She should be married to the child's father. And she knew Ben. He would make a good *daed* and husband. But could she make a *gut* wife for him? When she'd always love another man? A man who was his own brother?

Rachel flinched when the clock struck the hour, the sound overly loud in the silent room. Time was something she didn't have. She longed to wait on the decision, as marriage was for life. What if Aaron came back? But would he even marry her, knowing she carried his brother's child? The threat of nausea had her throat bobbing in a hard swallow. Flicking a piece of lint off her skirt, she shifted her hand subtly to rest against her stomach. She glanced across the room to the baby's father. Ben met and held her gaze. Again, so like him. Ben Raber would always be steady and true. Rachel drew in a deep breath, knowing whatever she might feel she needed to be fair to the two lives now connected to hers.

"Ja," she exhaled. *"Ja.* We're getting married."

Both the men in the room sighed, as well. Ben's was accompanied by eyes that drifted closed.

John Stoltzfus thoughtfully rubbed his hands together. "A sin confessed is a sin forgiven. As you've freely confessed and asked forgiveness of your sins, I don't see a need for this to go any further. The situation will obviously—" he grunted uncomfortably "—impact your wedding plans."

Rachel knew what he meant. They'd be punished, not directly, but subtly, through diminished celebrations. She also knew the minister's leniency had a great deal to do with the friendship he'd had with her *daed*.

Still, she was so relieved not to be placed under the *Bann* she almost slumped in her chair. Her lips twisted. Of course, her desire to collapse could be due to the perpetual tiredness that shadowed her lately. Only sheer will kept her on her feet some days.

As for the wedding, it wouldn't be the one she'd dreamed of anyway. Neither would the marriage. Nor the groom.

A glance at Ben revealed his dark head was bowed. Surely he was as relieved as she not to be placed under the *Bann*? Or had his sigh been more one of discouragement that he was now unexpectedly saddled with a wife?

Rachel bowed her head as well to hide the tears congregating behind her eyes. This couldn't be the marriage he'd hoped for either. How could they possibly make it work?

Chapter Three

"**W**hy do you keep watching the door? Everyone's here who can be here because of…" Rebecca flushed, "Well, you know."

Rachel grimaced as she sat with her sister, Ben and a few other *newehockers* at the *eck* table in the corner of her family's home. She certainly couldn't tell her sister she'd been watching the door in hopes Aaron would come through. Although now it wouldn't make any difference. It was too late. She'd said her vows to Benjamin this morning and she would never break them.

And yes, Rachel did know. Although they hadn't had to make a public confession in the few weeks since their visit to the minister, the smaller assembly was the district's way of punishing her and Ben for breaking the rules of the *Ordnung*. That, along with diminished festivities, fewer attendants and more limited decorations than she'd anticipated for her…other wedding.

All changes seemed insignificant to the fact that a different groom sat on her right at the corner table set up for the bridal party. She was Rachel Raber as she'd dreamed of for years, but she was married to a different Mr. Raber.

The reduced activities were intended as a disgrace for their sin, but Rachel didn't think she could be more shamed than when she'd had to face her *mamm* about the situation. Ben had offered to come in with her when they'd returned from seeing John Stoltzfus. Rachel had declined. It was time she left her youthful illusions behind and shouldered the responsibilities going forward. Besides—a flush rose in her cheeks—it would've made her more embarrassed to have him there.

Susannah Mast hadn't said anything. She'd looked up with a questioning smile when Rachel came through the door. As Rachel haltingly and tearfully explained where they'd gone and why, her *mamm* had slowly stood, her expression subsiding into a sympathetic frown. And then she'd opened her arms. Shaking with sobs, Rachel had walked into them.

There might be fewer sidesitters that joined her at the *eck* table than she'd planned to invite, but Susannah Mast had worked to ensure her oldest daughter had a memorable event. The farmhouse almost gleamed from intensive cleaning. Their corner table was laden with roast chicken, mashed potatoes and gravy, creamed celery, coleslaw, applesauce and fruit salad, with various desserts to be picked up from a side table later.

Rachel eyed the banquet before her ruefully. With fatigue and nausea continuing to plague her, she had little appetite for any of it.

Ben glanced over to give her a shy but supportive smile. His blue eyes were concerned when his gaze lingered on her barely touched plate.

He scowled. "Was it the mousetrap we found in the salad?"

Rachel's lips twitched at the common Amish wedding prank. "*Nee.* Actually, I was expecting something like that. Our friends have been known to pull a trick or two at these events."

"At least, as it's winter, hopefully they won't put the bed in the middle of the field." His eyes met hers. Rachel watched a flush that surely matched her own color his cheeks.

Ben suddenly found something of interest on his empty plate. "Well, I hope they won't."

Rachel cleared her throat, wanting to recall the brief moment of comradery. "I seem to remember being at weddings where you were an integral party to that activity."

With a rekindled twinkle in his eye, Ben returned his regard to her. "Probably more than my share. It seems to have gotten out that, as a furniture-maker, I'm pretty quick about disassembling and reassembling pieces wherever they might be needed."

Rachel was grateful for the shared smile. It was something she desperately needed today when she felt as if she were holding herself together with the straight pins that secured her wedding dress. When Ben's eyes softened, she found herself leaning imperceptibly closer.

"I meant to tell you that you look very…nice."

Rachel's eyes widened at his unexpected compliment. "I… *Denki.*"

Plain people didn't believe in using words like *pretty* or *beautiful* in regard to one another. To do so might make the recipient proud, or *hochmut.* Rachel soaked up Ben's words like a shriveled plant in a hot August. Affirmation, another thing she desperately needed today. It was something she'd really loved about Aaron. He'd showered her with positive comments all the time. But this was the first time she'd heard one from Ben. Warmth spread through her, permeating the edges of her tension and fatigue.

Reaching over, she touched his hand where it rested between them on the table. He inhaled deeply. Slipping his thumb away from his fingers, Ben shifted it to capture the tips of hers. The flare of warmth expanded. This was the first time they'd even held hands, if that's what they were doing. Rachel's heartbeat accelerated. He was her husband now. Her breath caught on the thought. *Her husband.* These past few weeks, she'd thought about getting married to Ben, not about being married to him. What would happen to their relationship after this afternoon?

The sound of a crash jerked her attention to the center of the room. A young man and woman stood glaring at each other, the dark liquid from a broken cup of coffee splattered over the linoleum at their feet, along with the fragments of white china. It was obvious the pair didn't get along. Which was regrettable, as they were husband and wife. It was common knowledge their relationship was as splintered as the porcelain scattered across the floor.

The warmth seeping into Rachel dissipated, replaced by a chill. The couple now the center of the room's attention started out the same way, for the same reason, as she and her new husband. She glanced at Ben's somber profile, his attention also fixed on the red-faced and thinned-lipped couple. Would the same happen to them?

"I hear they won't even be living together pretty soon," he murmured.

Rachel tugged on her hand. Ben's thumb tightened against the ends of her fingers for an instant before it fell away. Returning her hand to her lap, Rachel clenched it there in the folds of her blue wedding dress. A dress made when she was dreaming of a happy married life with another man. For the Amish, marriage was for life. If the relationship didn't work out, there was no way out unless one became a widow or widower. Please, please don't let them end up like the couple now assisting her *mamm* and other women in cleaning up the floor. Ben's hand remained on the table, tightened into a white-knuckled fist. How would she and Ben clean up the mess they'd made of their relationship?

Picking up her fork, Rachel prepared to take a bite of potatoes, just for something to do in the awkward situation. "I don't know if I ever thanked you for the china. It's a lovely set."

In lieu of an engagement ring like the *Englisch* did, an Amish man generally gave his intended something practical, like a clock or china. Along with the dishes, Ben had also presented her with a table and set of chairs he'd made.

"Hopefully that wasn't one of the pieces."

"Nee," she hastened to assure him. "My *mamm* had been collecting this china from resale shops this past year in anticipation…" Rachel's words dried up. The dishes had been collected in anticipation of her wed-

ding to his brother. She closed her eyes in frustration. Almost every topic led to a pitfall today.

Ben smiled wryly. "Your *mamm* was always wise that way."

Rachel strove to veer the conversation in another direction. "Well, she'll have them ready to share at a future barn-raising or community frolic."

Ben couldn't sit anymore. "I'm going to see if there's any coffee left. Can I get you something while I'm up?" Scooting his chair back, he shot to his feet. His mind had been constantly churning the past few weeks with regard to their future. The mention of a barn-raising reminded him of his next primary concern after the wedding. He had to find them a place to live.

New Amish couples typically spent the first several months at the bride's parents home while they established more permanent living arrangements. He and Rachel hadn't talked about theirs. Ben snorted as, wearing the expected smile for those he passed, he crossed the room to where the coffee urn was located. The two of them barely talked about anything.

Given the stiffness of their current relationship, Ben wondered how they'd survive one night, much less many months, living under someone else's roof without their stilted marriage becoming a community discussion. Not that Susannah would talk, but the Amish grapevine was such that the footfalls of someone limping across the floor on one side of the district echoed in conversations on the other side within a few hours, prompting folks to either whittle that person a cane or talk about how clumsy he was.

Ben didn't have the money to buy a place right now.

He hadn't expected to be married this soon. He'd figured that, after watching Aaron wed the woman he wanted, it would be a while before he could even imagine settling on someone to marry. But *Gott* had another design. Looking across the room, Ben's heart ached at the sight of his bride. He was thrilled to adjust his plans to *Gott*'s, but it would take time. Maybe a second job? He'd ask around, but still, it would be months at best before he could afford a place, even if one was available. And they'd need one with enough room for the *boppeli...* Ben's eyes widened at the reminder.

"I sure didn't see this coming. As soon as the one was out of sight, she latched on to the other. I don't think even ticks jump to another body that fast." The sharp female voice siphoned through the clatter of dishware and background hum of conversation in the room.

"Then you obviously weren't paying attention. Ben was making calf eyes at Rachel even before I was married."

Swiveling, Ben saw two women on the other side of the big coffee urn, their backs to him. He could tell from the color of their *kapps* that one was married while the other wasn't. A moment later, Lydia Troyer's profile was visible as she frowned toward the *eck*.

Ben pressed his lips together. He was surprised any single man, in or out of the district, had missed her attention. If there were a prize for flirting, she was the perennial winner, including, to his chagrin, him the day of the sugaring, when he'd welcomed her distracting company at first.

Lydia's sister had been more subdued in her flirtations, but apparently not subdued enough. She was the female member of the couple who'd broken the coffee cup. Ben's ears burned as he reminded himself that, like the story in the *Biewel*, he certainly couldn't cast the first stone.

What pained him more than the parallel of how the couple's marriage began was the current status of it and the corresponding fear he and Rachel would end up the same way. Ben's arm jerked, sloshing coffee over the edge of his cup. He'd seen how her gaze had constantly flicked toward the door during the marriage service this morning, obviously hoping his brother would show. He'd been watching for the same person as well, with the opposite desire. Switching the cup to his other hand, Ben snagged a napkin and dried the coffee from his fingers. They were married. He vowed to do whatever was necessary to make the relationship work.

Dropping the napkin in a nearby receptacle, he raised his voice so the pair on the other side of the table could hear him. "*Denki* for coming. I appreciate the…respect you're showing by celebrating with us on this special day." He propped a smile onto his lips, but he couldn't make it reach his eyes.

Whirling to face him, Lydia flushed until her cheeks were as red as her hair. "*J-ja, denki* for having us," she muttered, looking everywhere but at Ben. "*Ach*, looks like they're clearing this seating to get ready for the next. I should go…and see if I'm needed for help." Ducking away, Lydia headed for the kitchen. Ben watched to make sure the young woman didn't go near Rachel. With an embarrassed, conciliatory smile, Lydia's sister left, as well. Ben knew Lydia was a gossip, but she probably wasn't saying much more than a few others were about his unexpected wedding. His troubled gaze followed the two women into the kitchen before it shifted, equally concerned, to where Rachel sat at the corner table.

He almost jumped at the hand that settled onto his shoulder. Turning, he looked into the steady regard of his employer, Malachi Schrock. "You're a good man, Benjamin Raber. Nothing is going to change that. And if your bride doesn't know it now, she'll soon figure it out."

Ben tried not to be embarrassed that the man, who he greatly respected, had witnessed the previous exchange and apparently interpreted some of Ben's unease.

Reaching up, Ben patted the hand still resting on his shoulder. "*Denki.* Those words are the best gift I could have gotten today."

"Don't judge your situation by others. She's not Rachel and the husband isn't you." Malachi's fingers tightened reassuringly on Ben's shoulders before he dropped his hand. "And I've never known anyone to work harder than you to make things right."

Ben wished he had the confidence in himself that his employer had. Still, the words encouraged him as he made his way back to his bride.

Hours later, Ben stared at the wooden door to Rachel's bedroom. Should he knock? After today, as per Amish custom to live in the bride's parents' home, it was his bedroom too. Rubbing a hand over the back of his neck, he swallowed. It was a custom about to be broken.

He eyed the door's handle like it was a wasp nest he needed to stick his hand into. "We've already tossed some of the more essential ones aside." His mouth hooked in a rueful smile. It wasn't as if theirs was a normal marriage. If they were to make it one, it might be best to do so without an audience.

Ach, well, he'd solved the situation. Hopefully his… wife agreed.

His wife.

He tried the word on again, speaking it softly. His wife, Rachel Mast, now Raber. Ben's hands flexed as he acknowledged the realization of a dream. Now that was definitely something his wife wouldn't agree on. Which was why he would never tell her. Far better to be silent and appear a fool to her than to speak and remove all doubt. His mouth snapped shut at the sound of footsteps from inside the room. Nothing like having his wife open the door to find him talking to himself like he was *narrish*. Although it was crazy to have loved his *bruder*'s girlfriend. Even crazier to have married her.

Firming his shoulders, Ben rapped his knuckles on the wooden panel. The footsteps stopped, then…nothing. He held his breath in the ensuing silence. Was she going to leave him outside the door, feeling like more of a fool than he already did?

"Ja?"

Exhaling at the quiet word, Ben twisted the doorknob. He took one step inside and stopped short. If he'd felt breathless on the other side of the door, he now felt like the time he and his three brothers had climbed upon one of his *daed*'s Percherons. When they'd all fallen off, Ben had landed at the bottom, with his brothers piling on top of him. He'd had no air. He had none now either. He'd never seen anything as beautiful as Rachel, with her dark hair streaming down over the shoulders and the back of her white nightgown. His jaw dropped. Along with his breath, gone were any intelligent words he'd planned to say. He hastily stepped back into the hallway.

He remained rooted there until a soft, "Come in," drifted through the open doorway. When he warily stepped through, Rachel, pale of face, stood by the window. Her hair was pulled behind her and under the quilt that was now wrapped about her shoulders. She offered Ben a quavering smile.

"I…" He pointed awkwardly toward the hallway. "They told me to come up. For the night." He swallowed. "Which I did." His toes curled inside his shoes, newly purchased for the occasion. He probably couldn't sound more *dumpkoff* if he tried.

Shaking his head, Ben's lips twitched into a self-depreciating grin. "Obviously, becoming a husband hasn't made me any wiser. Except," his smile evaporated as his gaze flicked around the room, "that I don't think it's a *gut* idea for us to be here together while we're still…" he twisted his hand back and forth, searching for a word "…uncomfortable with each other." The look of surprise and relief that swept across Rachel's face was unflatteringly obvious. If he'd felt the same way, it would've been comical. Instead it was more evidence of the missing foundation necessary to build their relationship.

"So. After it gets quiet downstairs, I'll go out to the barn and spend the night."

Rachel's eyes rounded. "You can't do that. You'll get caught."

"I'll be careful, but it's only for tonight. After we help clean up from the wedding tomorrow, I'll start work on moving us into our new place."

"New place?" Rachel frowned, her brows lowered in confusion.

Ben hoped she wasn't too disappointed not to be traveling around the community over the next few weeks, calling on friends and collecting wedding gifts. She'd seemed strained enough just with today's events. Given the situation, he'd assumed she might want to avoid the other activity for now. It'd be difficult to hide that they weren't sharing a room if they stayed with everyone they visited, as was customary. He couldn't sneak out to all the barns in the community. She was right—it'd only be a matter of time before he was caught.

Which was why Ben was so excited about his news. He struggled to contain the enthusiasm in his voice. "*Ja.* I was just talking with Isaiah Zook. He recently bought an *Englisch* farm. It'll be a few years before any of his daughters are old enough to marry, so the house will be available for a while. He's moved his dairy steers and some of his Holstein bulls over from his own place, as he'll be expanding his cow operation there."

Ben had always enjoyed working with cattle. He couldn't believe their *gut* fortune. "In exchange for lower rent, we'll just need to do a few chores around the place. Isn't that *wunderbar*?" An economic place to live in private where he and Rachel could establish a stronger foundation for their marriage. It was more than he could've hoped for.

Sagging, Rachel braced a hand against the windowsill. Her face paled further until she was as white as the *kapp* sitting on the dresser beside her. Ben tightened his grip on the door handle to steady himself in the deluge of disappointment. Obviously, his wife thought living alone with her new husband was anything but *wunderbar*.

Backing out of the room, Ben pulled the door shut behind him as he stared blindly down the narrow hallway.

Chapter Four

Rachel cleared the breakfast dishes from the table as Ben finished the last of his coffee. They'd developed a routine of sorts over the last four weeks. She'd come out from her bedroom to start breakfast while Ben came out of his to head for the cattle chores. By the time he returned to the house, she'd have breakfast on the table. They'd eat a quiet meal together before he'd leave for work. In the evening, they'd do it in reverse. He'd come home, do chores and come in for a quiet meal before they'd head for their separate bedrooms.

Running water into the sink, Rachel snorted. Good thing the rental house had more than one bedroom, or maybe that'd been the plan. Ben had moved in the day after the wedding, with the excuse of needing to start taking care of the livestock. When he'd shown her the house, his jaw tight while he avoided her gaze, Ben had murmured that as things currently stood, he figured she could take the master bedroom and he'd use the one across the hall. Just until they got settled.

Whatever settled was. Apparently, they weren't there yet. Rachel felt a mixture of relief and…concern at the current situation. Surely this wasn't normal for married couples. It wasn't living in separate houses, but still... She certainly hadn't mentioned the discussion again, and neither had Benjamin.

Another thing he hadn't commented on was her tendency to break into tears at the drop of a hat. It frustrated Rachel, as she wasn't normally a weepy person, but for some reason, she couldn't keep the waterworks at bay. Whenever she started to cry, Ben's blue eyes would go solemn as he found her some type of tissue. But he never said a word. In fact, Ben hadn't commented on a lot of things, except to talk about the dreadful cattle and to tell her about his work at Schrock Brothers' Furniture when she asked.

Still, she found an odd sort of comfort having breakfast together before he'd harness Sojourner and head for town. It wasn't the marriage she'd dreamed of but, Rachel had to admit, it was better than she'd expected. It was tolerable. More, she had to admit, because of Ben's efforts than hers.

"What are your plans for the day?"

Rachel heard the scrape of his chair and the rattle of dishes behind her as Ben collected them to bring to the counter. He was always doing that. Taking care of little things she knew she should be doing. Rachel bit her lip, wondering if it was because he didn't think she was capable of keeping up with the housework by herself.

She squirted soap into the water. "I thought I'd be overly optimistic and plant some of the garden."

Ben's mouth curved in a small smile as he set his plate and cup on the counter. She'd told him of her delight in gardening and the canning associated with it later in the summer. Although he'd raised his eyebrows at the abundance of seeds she'd purchased, he'd borrowed a team and, with their landlord's permission, tilled up a large area on the place for her. "As long as you don't mind the risk of replanting if we get another frost."

"I'll take my chances." Anything to keep busy and not be constantly reminded of the large black-and-white cattle constantly milling about on the other side of the white rail fence beyond the driveway. And speaking of fences… "Why did you put up a fence in the garden?"

"Ach." To her surprise, his cheeks reddened. "I thought if you'd plant your cucumbers beneath it, the vines would grow up the woven wire. That way," Ben dropped a quick glance at her expanding waistline before rubbing the back of his neck, "you wouldn't have to bend over later this summer when it's…harder to."

It would make it a lot easier for her. Rachel blinked in surprise at his thoughtfulness. She wasn't used to that. While Aaron had showered her with sweet words, he'd rarely done something thoughtful like that for her. And Rachel hadn't expected it. Her *daed* had never done things like that for her *mamm*.

"Denki." She gave him a soft smile.

When she reached for his dishes, a flurry of activity outside the window caught her attention. A few of the cattle were wrestling with each other. Their roughhousing was standard activity. What wasn't normal was when the biggest one—a huge mostly black beast Ben had pointed out as the Zooks' prized young bull— used his broad head to butt a smaller steer in the pen. The steer was knocked onto its back into the wooden feed bunks that lined the fence. Rachel watched open-mouthed as four black-and-white feet flailed in the air.

"What is it?" Ben looked out to the window to see what had drawn her attention. "Oh, no!" He bolted for the door. Rachel followed in his wake to the front step and watched, wadding her apron in her wringing hands, as he sprinted toward the pen. Cattle scattered from along the fence as Ben vaulted over it, although a few, including the big black bull, didn't go far.

The bawl of the distressed steer cut through the chilly spring morning as Ben dashed to where it struggled in the wooden bunk. If he didn't get the animal off its back in time, the heavy weight of the steer's stomach would suffocate it. He couldn't abide the thought of losing an animal of his own. He definitely didn't want to lose someone else's livestock when he was responsible for it. Reaching the bunk, he tried to help the young Holstein get repositioned, taking a few kicks to the shoulder in their combined frantic efforts. It was no good.

Stepping back an instant to reassess, Ben's alarm increased as he heard the steer's breathing begin to strain. His eyes darted along the worn wood of the bunk. He had to break it to get the steer out. Now! Grabbing the top board with both hands, he jerked on it with all his strength.

"Rachel! Bring me the small chainsaw from the shed!" Splinters cut into Ben's fingers as he wrenched at the board. Although it moved a fraction of an inch, the nails groaning in their holes, he couldn't tug it farther. The steer emitted another pitiful bawl, weaker this time. Its white-circled eyes were bulging in its head.

"Rachel!" Ben spared a brief glance up to see, despite his urgent calls, his wife hadn't moved from the stoop. She wasn't going to help him. He didn't have time to race to the shed himself. The animal would be dead before he could get back. Frantically looking about for some type of tool, Ben spied the sledgehammer he'd recently used to pound in the steel posts for Rachel's garden. He'd set it down by the fence last night, intending to put it away when he finished chores, forgetting about it on his way to the house. Now the omission was his only chance to save the steer.

Dashing down the fence to where the hammer was propped against a post, Ben scrambled up the railings to lean over the fence top and grab its handle. With his adrenaline, the heavy head arced over the fence at his tug to bump, at the end of its swing, against the hip of an animal that'd come up to investigate the activity. Ben recognized Billy, the big young bull, as he raced back along the fence to the bunk where the steer struggled feebly.

Great, I let one animal die and injure Isaiah's prize bull. He'll probably kick me off the place. Positioning himself where his efforts wouldn't hit the trapped animal, Ben pounded away at the bunk's outer boards. To his great relief, after a few hard swings, the top boards moaned in protest before breaking away from the end of the bunk. Dropping the sledgehammer, Ben pushed them out the rest of the way. He jumped back into the bunk between the fence and the steer, who was laboring to breathe. Finding purchase, Ben groaned mightily as he wedged the animal out of the bunk. With the boards now gone, the animal tipped over the edge to drop the short distance into the churned mud of the pen, landing with its feet underneath it.

Ben sagged against the fence, gasping in unison

with the now freed steer. His legs were rubber. Sliding his back down the fence, he sat in what remained of the bunk as he anxiously watched the steer. When, after a tense few moments, the steer slowly lurched to his feet and ambled away, Ben closed his eyes in relief. When he opened them, Billy was watching him from ten yards away.

Figuring him as the culprit who created the situation, Ben admonished the young bull. "Don't do that anymore. He's no threat to you." Easing himself out of the bunk, Ben began to collect the pieces of the broken lumber while keeping an eye on the animal. Turning a back on a bull, particularly a dairy one, could get you killed. Any species of breeding male on a farm was always a danger, but bulls, with their size and unpredictability, were particularly dangerous. Dairy breeds, due to the way they were raised around people, were worse than beef bulls, because at maturity, they could perceive humans as their subordinate rivals.

Keeping a watchful eye on Billy, Ben ensured he'd accounted for all the nails that could've come loose with the boards. He didn't want one going up a hoof and injuring one of the cattle. With a last look at the young bull, he climbed over the fence. He needed to remind Rachel to keep well clear of Billy and the two other young bulls in the pen.

Glancing toward the house, he saw she'd gone back inside. Ben frowned as he carried the sledgehammer to the shed. He'd clearly requested Rachel's help. Hadn't she heard him? Was he expecting too much from her in her condition?

Or did her actions show she wanted him to fail? Did she want them to have to leave the farm and return to her mother's home? Was that what all the tears were about?

Or were they because he wasn't his brother?

With compressed lips, Ben headed to the barn to harness Sojourner. He was late for work. He may not be the one she wanted, but he was supporting her. At least that was something he could do right.

"Rachel." Ben spoke quietly from where he sat at the table following a quiet meal that evening, another in a string of quiet meals between the two of them over the weeks they'd been married. But this one had an added level of stiffness that made even *please pass the salt* an uncomfortable statement. What had they done to each other? Could they ever recover the easy comradery they'd had when they were young, or at least the somewhat amicable relationship they'd had when she was his brother's girlfriend?

At the sound of her name, Rachel's shoulders hunched where she stood with her back to him at the sink. Sighing, Ben steepled his fingers, tapping the tips of them against his mouth. He'd thought about this all day. This being their awkward relationship. Although he'd always dreamed of more, he'd thought they could at least work together enough in their marriage to make a reasonably comfortable life. Had he just been seeing what he wanted to see? Or did she actually want him to fail so she could justifiably think he was, and always would be, second best?

Closing his eyes, he took a deep breath. *Please let me say the right thing this time.* Opening his eyes, he studied her rigid back. "I'm sorry if I expected too much of you this morning when I asked for your help with the cattle."

Bowing her head, Rachel curled her fingers over the edge of the sink. "It wasn't that." The words, spoken to the window, were barely audible from where he sat.

"What was it then?" Sliding back his chair, Ben stood, bracing his palms on the table as he prepared to hear her lament that Aaron would never have let something like that happen, that everything would be better if only he'd been the one to leave instead of his brother.

Turning toward him, Rachel knuckled away a tear. "I just feel so foolish being an Amish farm girl who's afraid of cows."

"What?" Ben's weight sank onto his hands as he blinked in surprise.

Rachel sniffed. "When I was a little girl, I ran up too close to a cow and her newborn calf. The cow charged me. I've been petrified of them ever since."

What she confessed was so different from what he'd been expecting. Ben hissed out a shaky breath in relief.

"See? Even you think it's silly." Her lower lip quivered.

"*Nee*. Not at all." He straightened from where he'd slumped at the table. "I'm just so glad you told me what was bothering you. I can understand why you didn't want to come closer this morning." Circling the table, Ben approached where Rachel stood at the sink. Although he wanted to put an arm around her and draw her close, he settled for carefully cupping his hands about her tightly knotted ones.

"It probably would've helped to know this before I moved you onto a place where you have to face them every day." He tipped his head toward the window that looked out on the pen full of cattle. "I'm sorry. Is that why you're always crying? Because of the cattle? Is there some way I can help you work through your fear? Or…" he caught his breath "…do you want to move?"

"Oh, *nee*, we don't need to move." Rachel quickly shook her head, but the beginnings of a smile touched her face. "And," her cheeks pinkened, "I think the crying has something to do with the *boppeli*." She wrinkled her nose. "But, regarding the fear, I… I don't think I'm ready to confront it yet. I still feel a bit foolish about it."

Ben's heart rate sputtered when she twisted her hands to entwine them with his. "You shouldn't. We all have fears. Sometimes we know the reasons for them, sometimes we don't. Everyone is afraid of something. Even me."

Rachel rolled her eyes. "I can't believe that. You? The local hero? Who jumped into a frozen pond to rescue an *Englisch* boy who fell through the ice?"

Ben's lips twitched into a half grin. He'd forgotten about that day when he and Gideon Schrock had come upon the alarming situation. Thank *Gott* Gabe Bartel of the local EMS service had gotten there in time to resuscitate the boy after he and Gideon pulled him out. "I didn't have enough time to think of being afraid then."

He was delighted when Rachel's dark brown eyes teasingly narrowed under her delicate brows. "When you have time to think, what are *you* afraid of?" she challenged.

His smile evaporated. "Depends on the hour," he joked.

Ben's hands involuntarily tightened on hers before

he gently disentangled them and took a step back. His greatest fear was never far from his mind.

I'm afraid you'll never love me like you love my brother.

Chapter Five

"Have you seen her? It's growing more obvious by the day why someone had to marry Rachel so hastily."

Rachel paused beside the endcap displaying various boxes of crackers in the Bent 'N Dent store. Normally, she wouldn't have hesitated to move past other shoppers in the next aisle who were deep in discussion, usually with a reciprocating smile and nod, but in this conversation, her name was mentioned. And the conversation wasn't complimentary.

Things had been comfortable between Ben and her in the five weeks since the incident with the steer. While it was far from what she'd dreamed of, she could live with comfortable. Theirs may differ from a normal marriage, but she'd almost forgotten how it'd initially gotten started in the day-to-day work of keeping up a household, particularly during gardening season.

With that and dealing with her body acting in new and odd ways, she hadn't thought much about the community at large, other than to see folks at church. And be seen.

Rachel cast a self-conscious glance downward. Where

she'd always been slender as a reed, now it was apparent she…wasn't. While the Amish seldom spoke of a pregnancy, it didn't mean all were ignorant when confronted with an obvious one. Rachel hadn't considered what some in the community might think of her unexpected relationship turn. Her hands tightened on the handle of her basket as she blinked back tears. How did the old saying go? Eavesdroppers never hear any good of themselves?

Taking a step back, she was tempted to retreat to the far end of the aisle and slip past hopefully unseen. But then the speaker mentioned Ben's name. Rachel bit the inside of her cheek as she brushed a hand over the roundness under her apron. The community, or the few in it that liked to gossip, could say what they wanted about her, but she didn't want them saying anything about Ben. Whatever she'd expected when their marriage started, he'd been nothing but kind and supportive thus far. Indignation flared in her that he'd be maligned when he had ten, no, twenty times the character of the speaker. Sucking in a deep breath, she straightened her shoulders and stepped around the corner.

Already knowing whom she'd be facing as she'd recognized the voice, Rachel was prepared to meet Lydia Troyer with a bland smile. The smile wavered a bit when she saw the speaker's audience. She'd grown up with the young woman and thought of her as a friend. When the girl flushed redder than the coffee can behind her and murmured, "Sorry," before quickly excusing herself to hurry down the aisle, Rachel was reminded she'd only heard one person speaking. She'd been trapped a time or two in an unwanted conversation before. Now knowing how it felt to be the object of the discussion, she vowed to speak up and never be party to that kind of situation again.

Lydia flushed as well, but not as deeply. Rachel knew the young woman's embarrassment was due more to being caught gossiping than the gossiping itself. Still not accustomed to the roller coaster of her hormones, Rachel was grateful her tears had evaporated under a flash of heat directed toward the red-haired busybody who was discussing her private life.

"Please do go on, Lydia. I'm very curious as to what comes next."

Lydia's eyes widened in surprise at the unexpected comment from her supposed victim. Rachel's polite smile solidified. She knew she wasn't going to be able to prevent the girl from gossiping, but at least Lydia would know she wasn't going to be cowed by it.

Uncharitably, Rachel noted the red-haired woman's attractiveness greatly diminished when her mouth sagged like a carp instead of sporting her counterfeit simper. Of course, she wouldn't waste that on Rachel, who wasn't her preferred audience. Lydia snapped her mouth into a thin line as her eyes narrowed.

Rachel felt a moment of unease as her anger ebbed and threatened to take her courage with it. *Please don't fail me now.* Lydia's eyes darted to Rachel's midsection. Rachel braced herself.

"You didn't waste any time. Was that the way you tempted Ben to marry you?" Her expression slid into a sneer.

It was too close to the truth. Rachel's ears burned that someone else might overhear their conversation. She'd never been close to Lydia, although it hadn't been intentional. They'd interacted with other female friends while in school until eighth grade. Once out and into their *rumspringa*, Rachel had immediately coupled up with Aaron, while Lydia had flirted with anyone and everyone available in broadfall trousers. Rachel had noticed Lydia casting a few frowning glances in her direction at Sunday night singings and other functions, but she'd never thought the other woman actively didn't like her. Until now.

She dipped her chin to hide its trembling. "Whatever we've done, we've made our confessions. As to why, you'll have to ask Ben."

"One Raber *bruder* wasn't enough?" Lydia looked her up and down as if she didn't see anything special.

Shifting her feet, Rachel fought the urge to cross her arms over her middle. She didn't know why Aaron originally turned his attention to the shy, awkward girl she was when she entered her *rumspringa*. She'd just been dazzled that he had.

"If you and Aaron were such a pair, why didn't you go with him?"

Rachel furrowed her brows. "I couldn't. I'd been baptized. If I'd left, I'd have been shunned." Besides, Aaron hadn't asked. He hadn't even told her he was going to leave.

The other woman looked like she wouldn't mind shunning, if the recipient was Rachel. "There're few enough eligible men in the area. You didn't have to go rushing after Ben as a consolation prize, stealing him from other women. Maybe he had someone else in mind to walk out with before you flaunted yourself at him." Lydia's lips twisted. "But you didn't care."

But she hadn't gone rushing after Ben. She had just… Rachel caught her breath, recalling that awful

day. She had sought Ben out. When he'd seen her, he
hastened to determine the reason for her distress. He'd
received permission to leave work due to his *bruder*'s
unexpected departure. And her distraught self. Was
sobbing in someone's arms about his missing *bruder*
who happened to be her beau flaunting?

Ben had always been a friend, until he was relegated
more to Aaron's *bruder* while she and Aaron were dat-
ing. She hadn't paid much attention to what Ben was
doing at singings and such. She'd been totally absorbed
with Aaron. Had Ben been courting someone? Had he
been secretly walking out with another girl in the district? Rachel hissed in a breath. With Lydia? Surely
not? But he'd been with her that day in the woods while
sugaring. The day she'd finally advised him of her situation. With a troubled frown, she regarded the pinch-
faced woman before her.

Nausea, different from the normal kind frequently
troubling her lately, uncoiled in her stomach. Had she
unintentionally stolen Ben's future happiness with his
chosen one because hers had been yanked from her?
He'd never said a word.

But he wouldn't.

Rachel swallowed against the bile threatening the
back of her throat. Whatever Ben and her situation
was, it was now permanent. They were married. Even
if Lydia had been walking out with Ben before, the
relationship couldn't be changed. But it could be one
without joy. Particularly, if Ben had been interested
in someone else. As much as the thought troubled her,
and even as she knew she should forgive and forget,
Rachel couldn't give Lydia the satisfaction of feeling
she'd been successful in bullying her prey.

Though she was tempted, Rachel ensured her smile wasn't a gloating one as she lifted her head. "I care for Ben. No matter how we came together, we're now married. And nothing is going to change that." Glancing down into Lydia's nearly empty basket, she continued, "I hope you find what you're looking for."

With a slight nod, she turned and walked down the length of the aisle and over to the checkout counter. Whatever else she'd come into the store for was forgotten as her mind roiled with the realization she'd gone into this relationship thinking only of what she'd lost. She hadn't given any consideration to what her new husband might've given up.

Tossing her single bag into the buggy, she grimly climbed in behind it. She'd been proud of herself for thinking of the great job she'd been doing to tolerate the unfortunate situation she and Ben found themselves in. What if she wasn't the only one just trying to tolerate it?

Susannah Mast looked over from the goat pen as Rachel turned her horse into the lane. Rachel's shoulders slumped in relief at finding her at home. For some reason, the sight of her *mamm* brought her to tears. Snorting as she knuckled one away from her cheek, Rachel acknowledged almost anything could bring her to tears lately. So it wasn't surprising a little self-realization and guilt that she wasn't the only one in her marriage whose dreams had dissolved could turn on the waterworks. As had the guilt that, if disappointed, Ben had been doing a better job of making the best of it. Or at least appearing to do so.

Sniffing back the remaining tears, she drew the

horse to a stop and set the brake as Susannah secured the pen's gate behind her.

"This is an unexpected pleasure," Susannah called in greeting, a smile on her already sun-darkened face. Climbing down from the buggy, Rachel fought the urge to rush into her *mamm*'s arms. Instead, she strolled to the pen's fence to rest her elbows on the top rail.

"I was at the Bent 'N Dent and thought I'd stop by on the way home."

Having mirrored her actions, with her elbows resting on the fence beside her, Susannah raised her eyebrows. Rachel could understand. Her old home was far from a direct route between the store to where she now lived. With her husband. Who might be just tolerating their relationship. Her chin quivered. Stilling it with a frown, she focused on the multicolored goats in front of her.

"Kids all arrived for the year?"

She felt her *mamm*'s quiet regard before the older woman turned her attention to the pen. "Have a few stragglers. They should be coming soon." Susannah put a hand on Rachel's elbow. "You aren't here to talk about the goats. So what *are* you here to talk about?"

Turning to face the sympathetic brown eyes that matched her own, this time Rachel couldn't prevent her chin from quaking. "How did you guess?"

"I know my *dochder*. Do you want to stay out here with the goats, or would you like a glass of tea?"

"Tea would be nice." Rachel felt heat bloom up her neck. She cleared her throat as she tried not to touch her midsection. She knew her *mamm* knew, but so soon after the confrontation with Lydia, it was still embarrassing. Pivoting, she followed her *mamm* across the yard and into the kitchen. Here, amongst the familiar surroundings, tension immediately began to seep away. With shaky knees, she sank onto a worn kitchen chair.

Susannah retrieved a pitcher from the refrigerator and poured two glasses of tea. Setting one in front of Rachel, she pulled out a chair on the table's opposite side and sat down. After taking a sip of tea, she set down her glass, rested her hands on the table and gave Rachel an understanding smile. "It's a lot to adjust to in a relatively short period of time."

Rachel shook her head against the tears that again welled in her eyes. Lifting her apron, she dabbed at them, laughing without humor as she repeated, "How did you guess?"

"I was a new bride once. And an impending mother." Her lips twisted wryly. "And one quick upon the other, but not quite as quick as you."

Sniffing, Rachel put the apron to use again. "I don't feel quick at anything anymore." She gestured to her stomach. "Definitely not quick on my feet. Not quick keeping up with the garden and housework." Face contorting, she hitched in a breath. "And not quick to have anything more than an awkward companionship with my husband." Embarrassed at her outburst, she mopped up tears until the apron felt damp in her clenched hands.

There was an audible sigh from across the table. "You have to work at your marriage. You're two different people who suddenly formed a union, but you're two different people who now need to work together to make a single unit."

Rachel dropped the apron to meet her *mamm*'s compassionate gaze.

"You've driven draft teams before. Surely you've noticed the teams that pull together evenly get work done more efficiently and seem happier doing it. I know he isn't the one you thought you'd be in harness with. But that doesn't matter, you're a team now and there's no changing that. No matter what you feel for him, he is your husband, whether you care for him or not."

"I know that. And I do care for him."

"I'm glad to hear it, for he's a very *gut* man."

"It's just that…" Rachel didn't continue. She wasn't sure how to express her feelings.

"It's just that what?"

She should've known her mother would be persistent. "Well." She furrowed her brows. "With Aaron, I knew how he felt. And how he made me feel. He was always saying nice things to me. I liked that. Ben doesn't say much, and definitely doesn't use the sweet words that make me feel he cares for me, although he's always doing things for me."

"Saying nice things doesn't get the work done."

Rachel frowned. "*Daed* would always say nice things to you."

"*Ach.*" Her *mamm* shook her head. "As I said, saying nice things doesn't get the work done."

Rachel knew she must've looked as stricken as she felt, as Susannah hastened to continue. "Your *daed* and I loved each other. Have no doubt about that. But people show love in different ways. People look for love in different ways. Your *daed* was *gut* about telling me how the sunlight gleamed in my hair and how he appreciated all the work I did around the place." Susannah smiled ruefully. "But there were times that instead of hearing about my hair, I'd rather he'd have done more doing and less appreciating."

Rachel thought back on what she knew of her parents' marriage. There'd never been harsh words. But now she thought about it, when he'd been alive, her *daed* had been fishing many a morning when her *mamm* had been working with the bees or the goats. As Rachel knew the farm had come from her *mamm*'s father, she'd assumed that played a part in the work quotient. Now she wondered. She loved her *daed*, but his heart had seemed more in the ministry he'd later been selected for and less in the farming. Until now, she'd never heard her *mamm* say a negative word about him.

"I always liked it when *Daed* would mention how well I'd done at school. Or tell me how *gut* the meal was that I'd fixed while you were outside working." Rachel's confession was hesitant. "Or how *gut* a job I was doing taking care of Rebecca while you were with the *boppeli*." Her voice faded away on the last word.

Her expression falling into sorrowful lines, Susannah reached across the table to grab Rachel's hand. "I'm so sorry. I didn't think about what a burden it might've been for you when all my attention that wasn't on the farm while they were ill went to them."

Rachel returned the comforting squeeze. "I feel guilty remembering how his words made me feel appreciated when—" She stopped short at the stark look on her *mamm*'s face.

"When I didn't have time to even acknowledge your presence, other than to give you instructions for the day. You were young to be burdened so. I shouldn't have done that. We should've kept a hired girl longer. And I should've been the one to say *gut* words to you."

"It's all right, *Mamm*. I understood. I knew they needed you."

Susannah's eyes closed. She pressed her lips in a line that was as firm as it was fragile. When she spoke, her words were barely audible across the table. Rachel felt more than heard them. "We lost them anyway."

Rachel had been very young, but she still remembered the babies. First a little *bruder*, then about a year later, a little *schweschder*. So excited at first for a new *boppeli*, it hadn't taken long to see something was wrong. Even as newborns, when they'd open their tiny unfocused eyes, the backgrounds would be yellow, not white. Their skin was an unnatural golden. They both died very young.

It was only after they were gone that Rachel had heard the words *genetic disease* mentioned in hushed tones between her parents. Nothing more was said about the *boppeli*. The Amish way was not to grieve overmuch when someone dies, as to do so would be questioning *Gott*'s will. But for a long while, her *mamm* hadn't returned to the no-nonsense cheerfulness that usually personified her. The winter Rachel turned ten, she'd noticed Susannah had grown especially quiet. Rachel smiled, realizing now her *mamm* had been expecting her little *bruder*. Only after Amos had arrived, with enormous blue eyes in a perfectly white background, had Susannah brightened.

Rachel's breathing slowed. She hadn't thought of her lost siblings for years. Or the hereditary disease concerns the Amish were prone to, beginning as they had with a handful of families and usually marrying within their group, therefore limiting the gene pool. Pulling her hand free from her *mamm*'s loose grasp, she wrapped her arm protectively around the bump under her apron. "What if—" She cast a wide-eyed gaze across the table.

Pushing back her chair, Susannah circled the table to put her arm around Rachel's hunched shoulders. "*Ja*. There is a chance. But whatever happens will be *Gott*'s will. I've learned fretting about it doesn't help you or the *boppeli*. Has Ben spoken of any issues in his family?"

"*Nee*." Neither had Aaron. But they'd never talked about it. She and Aaron had talked of frivolous things about marriage, not thinking about *boppeli* at the time. And she hadn't mentioned her deceased siblings. To either of them. As they'd all been young at the time, they might not remember them.

"Well." Removing her arm, Susannah gave Rachel's shoulder a last pat and returned to her seat. "Whether the *boppeli* is affected is entirely up to *Gott*. The success of your marriage, on the other hand, is something you have an impact on. So what really brought you here today?"

Her *mamm*, as usual, was right. Their discussion about the *boppeli* had reduced to insignificance Rachel's distress over the confrontation with Lydia. "I just realized that Ben might not have wanted this marriage any more than I did at the time."

"And what brought that on?"

Rachel shrugged sheepishly. After their previous topic, it seemed so trivial. "I overheard Lydia Troyer talking about me in the Bent 'N Dent. About how I went so fast from one Raber *bruder* to another. About how someone had to marry me. Quickly." The words still stung.

Susannah huffed. "If my horse ran as fast as that girl's mouth, I'd get to town in half the time. The *Biewel* has something to say about gossipers. Why do you let her bother you?"

Rachel bowed her head. "Is it gossip if it's true?" She swallowed. "I did go very quickly from Aaron to Ben. And he did have to."

For a moment, the only sound in the kitchen was the ticking of a wall clock. "Has Ben given you any reason to think he didn't want this marriage?"

Rachel thought back over Ben's actions from the time she told him about the *boppeli.* She shook her head. *"Nee."*

"Benjamin Raber strikes me as one who knows his mind. You're married to a fine man. One who's no longer available to other single girls in the community. No wonder Lydia is upset. She's been dangling after anyone in suspenders since she got out of braids. She's seen girls younger than her make *gut* matches while with her, the available men shop but don't buy. She'll find something else to talk about before long. Besides, those who listen to such drivel don't matter and those who matter don't listen."

When Rachel raised her head, it was to meet Susannah's narrowed eyes. "You mentioned *at the time*. Not that you have a choice, but do I understand you want this marriage now?"

"As you'd pointed out, he is my husband." Rachel hunched a shoulder. "But, *ja*, I want it to be more than…more than what we have right now." Poking a finger in the condensation gathering at the base of her glass, she drew a short line on the table. "He doesn't say the words I liked to hear like Aaron did. But he

does things in his own way that are…special." Twisting her lips, she continued, "And as for work you mentioned earlier, it seems we're both working all the time. I don't see how we could be working any more."

"You're working. But are you working on your relationship? From the way your feelings are beginning to change, it sounds like Ben is. Are you?"

Rachel pulled another line of moisture from the ring at the base of the glass. She thought back over the past few months. Was she? She was tolerating the cattle. She didn't say anything more about them, but then neither had Ben since she'd told him of her fear. She thought of the work he'd done for her in the garden, and many other thoughtful things she'd never commented on. And she'd done…? Other than keep up with the housework and ensure there were meals on the table, had she reciprocated in simple thoughtful gestures? Or just absorbed his like a dried-up sponge?

Sighing, she leaned back from the table. She'd been selfish. Drumming her fingers on her stomach, Rachel reasoned she had the excuse she'd had many new things going on in her life. But so had Ben. But he'd been finding ways to put in extra, unselfish effort. It was time she did too.

She raised a wry glance to Susannah. "*Mamm*, how come every time I'm around you, you put me to work in some fashion?"

"Habit, I guess. Makes me wonder why you come around."

"Habit, I guess. And one I hope to never break. But now," Rachel pushed up from the table, "I need to go home and," she wrinkled her nose, "work."

Rachel was surprised at the moisture that seemed

to glimmer in her *mamm*'s eyes as she also stood. "I'm sure you'll do as well there as you always did here. And I'll be just as proud."

Minutes later, after a final wave, Rachel gathered up her bay's reins and directed him down the lane. Encouraging words from her *mamm* might've been rare while growing up. But, Rachel smiled broadly as her heart swelled, she couldn't imagine they would've felt any better than those few words did right now.

Now to go home and apply her *mamm*'s advice. And wonder if Ben would notice her efforts.

Chapter Six

Who knew that concentrated effort on her marriage would begin with a trip to the feed store the next day? When Ben tentatively asked as she was cleaning up the breakfast dishes if she'd like to ride along, Rachel figured it was the closest she could get to doing something with him regarding the wretched cattle while staying far away from the beasts. Regardless of her motivation, they'd barely turned out of the lane when the beauty of the late spring day called to her, making her glad she'd come. That and the shy smiles her husband kept sending in her direction. Although their conversation centered on the clear, sunny sky after the previous week's rain and the blooming vegetation along the side of the road, it was as pleasant as the lovely weather.

They ran into Gideon Schrock, Ben's coworker at Schrock Brothers' Furniture and good friend, coming out of the feed store as they went in. He stayed around to help load the bags of soybean meal pellets Ben was picking up on Isaiah Zook's account into the flat back of the open buggy Plain folks in the area used in warmer weather.

When the men had stacked the last of the bags, Gideon leaned on the top one as he considered them. "You two have lunch plans? If not, would you like to join me at The Dew Drop?"

Ben, after a glance at Rachel, declined his friend's invitation to join him at the town's main restaurant with a regretful shake of his head. "*Ach*, as I did chores first this morning, we're not that long up from the breakfast table. Also, as this belongs to Isaiah, I want to get it safely put up in the barn before there's any chance the weather changes. Besides," he secured the short board across the end of the wagon, "fine as the cooking is at The Dew Drop, Rachel's is better."

Gideon turned to her with a smile. "High praise indeed. I hope you have a touch for frying mushrooms. They're one of Ben's favorite foods. I'm surprised he didn't give a test on fixing them before you two were married."

Rachel flushed. There hadn't been a discussion on cooking skills, much less anything else besides the forthcoming *boppeli* when she and Ben had determined to marry. She smiled tepidly in response to Gideon's teasing. Not fond of mushrooms to begin with, as touchy as her stomach still was months into her condition, the memory of the edible fungi's heavy smell while cooking made her ill. The thought of frying morel mushrooms several times during their current growing season made her want to run behind the store and retch.

She swallowed against the growing nausea. Her *mamm* had advised she needed to work on her marriage in order to make it succeed. Right now, success would be getting her and Ben back to a comfortable friendship. If that meant holding her breath and ignoring her rebellious stomach while she cooked what was her husband's favorite food, it was a start. At least walking in the spring-growth woods together would be pleasant. And frying up his favorite food—Rachel tipped her face away and managed to control her grimace at the thought of the smell—could definitely be considered work on her part.

When she turned back, she found her husband watching her. "Would you like to go mushroom hunting? I know a good spot to find them." He glanced at Gideon. "A location I'll never divulge."

Sighing inwardly, Rachel propped up the corners of her lips into a smile. "*Ja.* Sounds *gut.* Do I have to keep it a secret too?"

Gideon nodded. "First rule of a good marriage is to not reveal the location of secret morel patches."

Given the situation of their marriage, the absurdity of the requirement made Rachel's lips twitch for real. Rules of a good marriage? How about not to expect a *boppeli* with your intended brother-in-law before getting married? She wasn't sure, but probably sleeping in the same bedroom once wedded might be a candidate for the list. Maybe talking with your spouse more than *please pass the salt* or a stilted *how was your day?* might be included. In all likelihood, it wasn't a rule, but not being terrified of something your husband enjoyed would be helpful.

Even though she'd prefer to have the whole church district and some of the *Englisch* neighbors as well tramp through the secret mushroom-hunting ground so there would be none to find, take home to prepare and—she shuddered—eat, if it would help in laying the foundation of a good marriage with Ben, she'd go find, cook and try to eat a mushroom.

"My lips are sealed." Reaching up, Rachel tapped her mouth. A glimpse at Ben revealed his attention was lingering on her lips where her fingers rested. The look in his blue eyes made her grateful there was a spring breeze that stirred against her heated cheeks. He looked away when she lowered her hand.

On the way home, Ben gave her an out. Keeping his eyes directed on his horse Sojourner, he murmured, "We don't have to go if you don't want to. I've got work I can do around home."

Although instantly tempted, Rachel responded. "*Nee*. Sounds like fun. It looks like a lovely day to walk in the woods." *You'd be proud of me, Mamm.*

Ben looked more excited than she'd seen him in some time. "Sounds *gut* then. If you want to grab some baskets and knives, we'll go as soon as I unload the feed."

An hour after reaching home, Ben was filling her in on mushrooms as they approached his clandestine hunting grounds. "When the daytime highs are in the sixties and the lows stay above forty degrees, the morels start coming out." They pulled off the county blacktop onto a short well-shaded lane. Fifty yards farther, Ben drew the bay mare to a halt in a small clearing. Scanning the area for some place to secure Sojourner, he continued talking. Rachel suspected he knew she didn't have that much interest in the topic, but she appreciated his enthusiasm and efforts at conversation, preferring it over their continued silences.

"They like well-drained sandy soils. And areas around oaks, ash and elm trees. A lot of times, they grow around dead or dying trees. I look extra close if I see an area where the bark is slipping off the trunk." He guided Sojourner to a small bush among the trees that ringed the clearing. Snagging the lead rope, he climbed down to secure the mare to one of its branches.

Grabbing the two baskets they'd brought along for the mushrooms Rachel hoped would stay empty during their exploration, she joined him. Sojourner was already nibbling on the bush when Ben relieved Rachel of one of the baskets. "Just keep your eyes on the ground. Once you find one, slow down and search the area carefully. There're probably more."

That's what she was afraid of. Rachel didn't mind the hunting of mushrooms. It was the thought of soaking whatever they found in water for a couple of hours to clean them and wash out any bugs living inside the hollow mushrooms that made her shudder. That and the reaction of her currently delicate stomach to the strong smell as they were sautéed or cooked however Ben might prefer.

But I'm trying, Mamm. She had to admit, it was less awkward between them as they were actually doing something instead of avoiding eye contact across the table. Besides, it was a pretty spring morning to walk in the woods.

Last fall's leaves rustled as Ben shuffled through them a short distance beyond her. Rachel kept her attention on the ground, more so to not trip over a branch than to find a mushroom. She wasn't looking hard for morels and didn't expect to find any.

But there, between her right foot and the deteriorating wood of a fallen log, she instantly recognized the tall honeycombed cap and stem. A closer scrutiny of the surrounding area yielded several more. Tightening her grip on her small basket, she stole a glance at Ben. With the downed log between them, he couldn't see the small but bountiful patch. Rachel gnawed on her lip. With the toe of her shoe, she nudged some surrounding leaves and bits of bark around the area until even the tips of the mushrooms were barely visible.

She jumped when Ben called from where he was searching roughly fifteen yards away. "Finding anything?"

"N-nee." Rachel inched away from the now-concealed mushrooms.

"That's funny. This is usually a pretty good spot for hunting."

"Maybe it's still a little early for them?" she offered halfheartedly as she angled away from the fallen log.

"Maybe. Might have to come up with something else for supper."

"I'm sure we'll think of something." The words couldn't tumble out of Rachel's mouth fast enough.

Ben rubbed a hand over his mouth and chin to hide his smile. It still startled him to find the beginnings of a beard, identifying him as a married man, every time he touched his face. A furtive glance in Rachel's direction ensured she was facing away. With his booted foot, he carefully shifted leaves over the prolific gathering of morels before him. He didn't think Rachel would search this way, but just in case, he camouflaged the earth's bounty.

He'd seen her kick leaves over the patch she'd found. His grin widened. He'd been wrong in his expectations for their outing. He'd figured Rachel wouldn't try too hard. She was trying hard all right, trying hard not to find any. Well, two could play at that game.

Her face had turned a bit green at the mention of frying mushrooms. The past few months, he'd watched her blanch at the smell of certain foods before hurrying to the bathroom. Causing her distress was the last thing he wanted. But she'd agreed to come. Ben had been surprised and encouraged. *Ach*, more than encouraged, he was thrilled.

And she seemed to be enjoying herself. Ben nudged some leaves over another trio of morels. So was he. Immensely enjoying not finding mushrooms with his wife.

Compared to what it could be, while not good, things had been all right between them these last few months. When he didn't see Rachel in profile, he'd even forget the original reason they married. Although she'd often try to hide them, he'd noticed a decrease in the frequency of her tears.

Even if they didn't share a bedroom, at least they were still living in the same house, unlike the couple from the wedding. Word was Lydia's sister and her children were in their farmhouse, while her husband had moved into the *daadi* house on the place, usually reserved for the older generation once the grandparents are ready to move out of the main house.

Ben didn't like gossip. He figured one shouldn't talk about someone what you wouldn't say to them. But when he'd heard the couple's woes mentioned, he'd pricked up his ears, as the fear of a similar fate in his marriage was a frequent companion.

So he was satisfied their relationship could be defined as all right. To intentionally try to change that brought risk. Risk he wasn't prepared to take. He glanced over to where Rachel was shuffling along through last autumn's fallen leaves, now with a stout walking stick in her hand. His lips twitched at the possibility she was using the stick to press mushrooms back under the leaves. Although he winced at the loss of a tasty mushroom, he was charmed she'd think of that. Charmed that she cared enough to come today. Charmed enough to express his feelings to her?

The prospect made his heart pound. Taking a couple deep breaths, he reminded himself he was fortunate for what he did have. They were married. It was more than he'd ever imagined. *Don't risk it.*

Ben grimaced. Because he'd saved the boy in the pond, folks thought he was brave. Those things were easy. He had no fear of risking his life or limb. But his blood ran cold at the thought of risking his heart. Of expressing feelings that could be ridiculed or not reciprocated.

So he couldn't say things. He wouldn't say things. But he couldn't help but show his feelings. Hopefully Rachel wouldn't notice. She never said anything about the things he did for her. Maybe she didn't care. He could live with that. He didn't want to think about not living with her. Or living with her pity if she didn't feel the same way.

"I thought you were supposed to be such a *wunderbar* mushroom hunter." Rachel made an exaggerated swing of her basket to display its emptiness.

"Must be the company." Ben grimaced comically as he turned his own basket upside down.

"Well, I guess I'll have to provide then. I think I'll be able to at least find some eggs when we get home so we won't starve. Would you like them fried, boiled or scrambled for supper?"

As they approached the clearing where they'd left the buggy, Ben figured his grin couldn't stretch any wider. Instead of enduring Rachel's teasing, he was relishing it. This was the Rachel he'd grown up with. The one he'd fallen in love with. Not the quiet, subdued Rachel he'd lived with the past several weeks, although he'd admired and respected that woman. And, he sighed with satisfaction, this was the way she'd acted around his brother, whom she'd loved. Was it possible she was growing to care for him?

"We'll have to see how many eggs you actually find. You might walk by a dozen right under your feet." As had been the case with the morels. His secret spot had been so prolific with them, the challenge had been guiding her away from the patches without either of them admitting they saw the iconic mushrooms.

He blinked against the sunlight as they left the shade of the budding trees.

Rachel stopped and glanced around the empty clearing. "Speaking of finding, are you sure we found our way back?"

"Ja," Ben said as he surveyed the area, as well. He was certain of it. But a horse and buggy were pretty difficult to miss. Where had Sojourner gone? Walking the perimeter of the empty clearing, he found proof of where the rig had been parked. Fingering the now stripped bush, Ben discovered the method of her escape. He wiggled what was left of the branch of the bush he'd tied the mare to.

"Ach. Looks like she chewed herself free. I should've secured her better." He'd never made a mistake like

that before. But his mind at the time had been on the encouraging smiles of his wife and the hopes those smiles had wrought.

He ran an assessing eye over Rachel as he considered the situation. While she'd seemed fine for their tromp through the woods, he didn't know how long they might now be on foot. He didn't want to tire her out. Rachel was tall, but even so, there was extensive rounding under her apron. Ben squinted at the sight, trying to recall how many months with child she would be. Three? *Nee*. It would be slightly more than four now.

His eyes narrowed further. Ruth Schrock, his boss's wife, had delivered a baby girl early this year. Although no one spoke of the pregnancy, Ben remembered when she'd come in to visit the business where she'd previously worked. Ruth was a much shorter woman than Rachel. Still, there'd not been a suspicion she was with child until much closer to when the baby had been born.

By his calculations, Rachel's child would arrive in the fall. And a profile of his wife already indicated there was no question about her condition. Why would she be so advanced? Frowning, he mentally counted the months again. He froze as Rachel's words that day when they were tapping the maple trees came back to him. She'd said she was having a *boppeli*.

She didn't say she was having his *boppeli*.

Was it possible…

"How far do you think she went?"

He flinched at Rachel's question. She was frowning now, as well. Ben shook off his troubling thoughts.

Right now, the priority was to find their transportation. And equally important to him, regain Rachel's smiles.

He propped up the corners of his mouth. "*Ach*, fortunately for us, she should be easier to see than the morels were. But I don't know how long she's been gone or how fast she was going. Do you want to stay here in the shade and wait for me to come back with her? Hard telling how far she went."

Rachel dipped her chin shyly. "I'd rather go with you."

Ben smiled at the admission, but he hesitantly nodded toward her middle. "Are you sure you feel up to walking some more?"

"*Ja*. I'm *gut*."

"Well, at least in this, you don't have to even think about bending over. Although perhaps we'll find more mushrooms on the road than we did in the woods."

Bumping his basket with hers, Rachel smiled at his teasing. "I'll let you get them then."

They turned in accord toward the lane on the far side of the clearing. Ben shifted his basket to his outside hand and let the other one dangle between them. "Think she went all the way home?"

Rachel's eyes widened, probably thinking as he was of the several miles distance. "I hope not." She bit her lip. "Is she an ambitious type?"

Ben thought of his mare. "Not generally. She has a nose for good grass though. I'd even have called her a picky eater." He grinned again. "Until she ate the scrub bush."

To his delight, his wife grinned back at him. "Maybe it was an intentional escape." To his further delight, she shifted her basket to her outside hand. Her now free one brushed against his as they started under the tree canopy of large oaks that draped over the lane.

"Hmm. I don't know. Hopefully it doesn't become the fugitives of the farmyard. What next? The cows?"

Rachel giggled at his bad joke. Their hands brushed. And lingered together. Ben hooked his little finger around hers. His heart beat accelerated when she didn't resist. Or let go. "Of course, that might not be something you get too upset about."

"Now, I disagree on that."

Ben's grin faded at her serious tone.

"I'd be highly upset if they came into my garden instead of heading down to the road," she continued.

"Can't have them walking through the zucchini. I'll check the gates. And if Sojy's become an escape artist, maybe I better check the hitches around the community. She might choose to use one of the wooden posts for a toothpick."

Rachel giggled again. When they'd walked out of the woods to find an empty clearing, she'd held her breath. She was prepared for what Aaron's response might have been confronting the situation. It likely wouldn't have been Ben's comic banter and the two of them giggling together like children on an outing. What normally would've been undesirable circumstances was actually fun, because of the man beside her. Granted, her feet hurt and she was tired. But what had started out as something of a chore had turned into a joy. Rachel slanted a glance at her husband, her lips lifted at his engaging profile. Of their own seeming volition, the rest of her fingers eased into his until their clasped hands swung easily between them.

Maybe when you worked at marriage, it didn't seem like so much work after all.

Fortunately, they hadn't gone much more than half a mile when they saw Sojourner in the distance, halfway up an *Englisch* farmer's lane, her head down as she grazed on the lush green lawn that lined it.

"We've found the fugitive."

"Is her choice of farm going to give us any problem?" Rachel was apprehensive. Some *Englischers* weren't fond of having Amish neighbors.

"*Nee*. It's *gut*. I know this farmer. He won't have a problem. If he's home, he'll just probably tease me about our predicament."

"You don't think she's considering leaving the Plain life for the *Englisch* one, do you?" Rachel looked up at Ben, expecting him to joke back. She watched the amiable expression fade from his face at the same time he loosened his hand from hers to flex his fingers and let it swing at his side.

"*Nee*. She's got a good life with the Amish. Besides, her Pennsylvania Dutch is much better than her English." He paused, before adding in a quiet murmur. "And she'd let me know if she had plans to leave."

Rachel's brow furrowed at his abrupt change. Until she remembered who'd left for the *Englisch* life without telling anyone. Aaron. She stumbled, bumping into Ben before she recovered her balance. How could she have forgotten? His departure was what'd prompted the basis of her life now. She loved the man. Something she'd totally forgotten while basking in an unexpectedly delightful afternoon with her husband. But why was she feeling guilty? Shouldn't she be forgetting

Aaron? He couldn't be a part of her future. But he'd been so much a part of her past. Years of it. And she'd forgotten because of the man beside her.

She was trembling when she felt Ben's strong grasp under her elbow. "Are you all right?"

"*Ja*. Just…tired." When Ben swung her up into his arms, she gasped. "You shouldn't! I'm too heavy," she protested.

"I should've thought of this before." Ben adjusted his grip to hand her his basket before shifting his arm back under her knees. "And you're no heavier than some bales of hay I've thrown."

Rachel had to admit, it was a relief to be off her feet. "I feel like I'm shaped like one. I'm huge." Her face was close to his shoulder. From his shirt, a whiff of the soap she used for laundry, warmed by the man wearing it, drifted to her. Blushing, she retained a grip on the basket handles in one hand, resting them over her rounded stomach as she looped her other arm around the back of his neck for support.

The muscles of Ben's neck stretched under her hand as he looked down. Rachel glanced up with a tremulous smile, expecting to share it with Ben. His pensive expression as he considered her midsection sent a chill through her. When his blue eyes met hers, they were troubled. He abruptly looked away. Startled by his reaction, Rachel remained quiet as they closed the distance to the lane.

Fortunately, Sojourner didn't wander farther as they approached. Ben situated Rachel in the buggy and they drove up to the house. The *Englisch* farmer wasn't home. Rachel wished he had been. At least then it might have prompted a conversation during the quiet ride home when her husband's eyes repeatedly flicked to her stomach.

Chapter Seven

A boppeli. Not *his boppeli.*

Rachel's words when she'd first told him of her condition that day in the maple grove were all Ben had been able to think about for the past week.

He'd never thought about them before, realizing after what they'd done, the situation was possible. At her concern regarding her size last week when he'd picked her up, and after furtive glances since then at her profile, he did now. Was her pregnancy further along than he thought?

If that was the case, it couldn't be his child.

It was Aaron's.

His wife was going to have his brother's baby.

Ben shifted his position so he could look over Gideon Schrock's shoulder to watch Rachel, several yards away, as she, along with other women of the district, began removing the side dishes from the table after the picnic's stragglers had gone through for their second or possibly third helping. His lips felt bloodless, compressed as they were in a line firm enough to build a barn upon.

It wasn't the surprise that hollowed him to the core. It was…disappointment? But what had he expected? He'd stolen his brother's girl. Now he'd stolen his brother's life. And whatever happened, that couldn't change. Marriage was for life. Aaron, wherever he was, might be a father someday, but not to this one, his oldest child.

Shifting his eyes toward Gideon, Ben noted that although his friend nodded in response to whatever the two men standing with them were saying, he was frowning in Ben's direction. Lifting a hand to his mouth to cover it and rub his tight jaw, Ben nodded distractedly, as well.

It was Aaron who should be experiencing the wonders of seeing his wife grow with their child. Who should be experiencing the joys and fears that come with pending fatherhood.

But Ben would raise this child the best he could, no matter who the father was. Because he loved his brother. And loved the child's mother.

Ben couldn't blame Rachel for what she'd done. With his brother gone, she'd been in a terrible situation. Even if she hadn't told him, he'd have asked her to marry him as soon as he'd realized the circumstance. And she hadn't lied to him. He'd been the one to jump to conclusions. After that initial shocking announcement, they really hadn't talked much about the baby. There'd been so many other things to do.

"Everything all right?"

Ben blinked when Gideon placed a hand on his shoulder. Glancing about sheepishly, he realized the other two men who'd been with them had drifted away. He flushed under Gideon's raised eyebrow regard.

"It's okay. We just figured you were a man with a pretty bride and a…pending life change."

"You could say that," Ben murmured rueful agreement.

Gideon's eyes narrowed as he considered his friend. "You're not happy?"

Ben made sure he was smiling when he met his friend's concerned gaze. "*Ja.* Just a lot to think about."

Gideon dropped his hand. "*Ach.* You have cause. Lot of changes within a few months. It even surprised me when you two married. You'd never mentioned Rachel once between the time Aaron left and the wedding was announced in church. Believe me, I would've remembered, because you never talked about any girl."

Ben's smile was getting harder to keep in place. "Sometimes things just take us all by surprise." He debated sharing his concerns with Gideon, a coworker who'd become a *gut* friend. This recent discovery was feeling like a heavy burden to bear. He needed to discuss it with someone. Whereas before—with everything except the topic of Rachel—on the rare occasions he felt moved to speak of what was bothering him, he'd talk with Aaron. It hadn't been an option, for various reasons, on this topic.

A quick glance around confirmed no one was within listening distance. Inhaling deeply, he opened his mouth to divulge his apprehensions, only to close it again as he watched his younger *schweschder* hurrying toward them with a disturbed look on her face.

Gideon turned when Sarah joined them. She glanced briefly at the blond man before giving Ben a look that indicated she needed to speak with him. Alone. As it was out of character for the young woman, Ben furrowed his brow in her direction but didn't hesitate.

"Gideon, be glad you don't have *schweschder* here to nag you. I'm sure it's some task she wants me to do. I don't know why my younger *brieder* can't address whatever needs to be done, but as she's come to me, I'll assume it's because I'm the one who'll have to take care of it."

"That's all right. Actually, I wouldn't mind having my *schweschder* move up from Ohio. They haven't said anything, but I'm beginning to feel like a third wheel with Samuel and Gail, when they're more interested in a two-seater cart. With a place for Lily, of course. And I'm thinking, if they're wanting an extra mouth to feed soon, it's not me they have in mind. If Miriam came, maybe we could find a place together."

Sarah rolled her eyes at his friend's words. "You just want her to take care of the house and cook for you."

Gideon grinned. "Well, that did come to mind first."

Sarah turned her back on him to look meaningfully again at Ben. He'd been glad of their banter. It'd helped him relax. But he took her hint. "Seems this is a private discussion. I'll catch up with you later."

Gideon tipped his head in farewell. Ben watched him saunter off to join another group of men before turning his attention to his sister. "What's so important it couldn't wait nor have an audience?"

"I assumed you'd want to know that Lydia is telling all who will listen, and loud enough that those of us who don't want to will hear it anyway, that Rachel—" Sarah paused. Her eyes dropped as color rose in her cheeks.

Tension seeped into Ben. He straightened from his previously casual stance. "That Rachel?" he prompted.

"That Rachel…" She faltered again, her head still bowed. Drawing her shoulders back with a deep breath, she lifted her head. Her blue eyes were fierce when she met Ben's troubled gaze. "That it's Aaron's."

Ben felt like when he'd accidentally bumped up against an *Englisch* neighbor's electric fence. He blew out a steadying breath. It was one thing for him to speculate, to know, about his and his wife's situation. To even think about sharing it privately with a close friend. It was quite another for someone, whose business it wasn't, to be sharing it about the community.

"Did Rachel hear?"

Sarah shook her head. "I don't think so. She wasn't in the area, at least not when I was around."

Ben discovered his fists were clenched. He carefully extended his tightly curled fingers. "Where is Lydia?"

Sarah's worried glance moved from his face to his hands.

"It'll be fine. Where is she?"

"Before I left to find you, I heard her say something about taking dishes to her buggy."

He nodded. "*Denki* for telling me. You did the right thing," he reassured her. Knowing she was troubled about the situation, Ben reached over and awkwardly patted her shoulder. Sarah was the next oldest behind him and Aaron. The three of them had once been close. Maybe instead of talking with Gideon, he should be talking with her. But, his mouth settled into a grim line, right now, he needed to be talking with someone else.

With one last pat on Sarah's shoulder, he pivoted and strode toward the field where the buggies were parked.

He caught up with Lydia between the rows of black buggies as she was heading back toward the picnic area. To his relief, she was alone. Although, with as much as she'd apparently been talking, what he was going to discuss with her wouldn't be news to anyone. Still, he'd rather have his say in private.

The look on Lydia's face when she saw him revealed the red-haired woman had no idea what was on his mind. Ben didn't understand. Had she no shame, greeting him with an eager smile when she'd just been gossiping about his wife and *bruder*? Didn't she know he would take care of his family? With a few quick glances, she apparently noted their solitude and her smile shifted, giving Ben a look that implied she wanted him to forget the vows he'd made before *Gott* to his wife.

Ben was left a little breathless with shock. He'd never betray Rachel that way. He knew Lydia was a flirt. There'd been ample evidence over the years of her *rumspringa*. But he'd never thought she would extend her activities to that level. He stopped behind one of the buggies in the long rows that stretched across the field. The triangular orange and red sign hanging on the buggy's back reminded him to go slow, be cautious, as he watched the young woman sashay closer.

If she was willing to tempt him, a married man, did that indicate she might have no qualms as a married woman forsaking her own vows? Lowering his brow, Ben frowned. He'd never taken Lydia's attentions seriously, as he'd always had his eye on Rachel. But some of the other targets of her flirtations were his friends. Although his own marriage was far from ideal, he didn't want to think of his friends being trapped in a relationship like one with Lydia might be.

"Ben, what a pleasure to see you," she cooed, stopping a few feet away.

"You might not think so after our discussion."

"Oh, I doubt that." Stepping closer, she placed a hand on his shirt.

Ben jolted in surprise. He knew, unless someone else was out in the field, the buggies blocked anyone seeing them from the picnic area. But still, he was dismayed by her boldness. Encircling her wrist with careful fingers, he pulled it from his chest. "Stop gossiping about my wife."

Lydia batted her eyelashes and dropped her jaw in attempted innocence. "Has she been complaining? If folks are discussing her…hasty romances, it has nothing to do with me."

Releasing her wrist, Ben wiped his hand on his sleeve like he'd touched something unpleasant in the barnyard. "You're right. It has nothing to do with you. So that's enough. And if anything more is said, I'll know where it came from."

To his relief, she dropped the guile. "Why are you defending her? From the looks of it, it's not even your own *boppeli*." Her lips twisted into a sarcastic smile. "I forgot. Just like always, Ben comes along to fix what his older *bruder* left undone. Don't you ever get tired of it?"

A fireball of suppressed emotions erupted within Ben. Guilt, shame, fear, protection—he felt the sting of them all. Knowing she'd notice and gloat if he showed any reaction, he kept his expression neutral and hands loose. Catching his tongue between his teeth, he inhaled and released a quiet breath. "I get tired of worrying that my friends or younger *brieder* would be fool enough to walk out with you. Makes me think I'll have a little discussion with them. Remind them that just because the fish are practically leaping out of the pond to bite, it doesn't mean anything you snag is worth keeping."

The smile faded from her face.

It was an improvement, but not enough. "Almost wish I were still going to Sunday night singings, just to see everyone be too wise to give you a ride home at the end of the evening."

Her eyes narrowed. "I'll tell my *bruder*."

Ben worked with Jacob Troyer at Schrock Brothers Furniture. Although not close friends, he respected the man. "Go ahead. I'll tell him what you've been saying about my family." Ben was slightly embarrassed about the sharkish smile that lifted his lips. "And what some of my friends have been saying about how eager you are for the rides home."

Along with being surprised that she still could, he felt a little bad when her face flushed. The comment had been a reach—his friends weren't ones to kiss and tell—but either Lydia didn't know that, or had done more than he knew with them, and others. He figured the latter. "No more talk about my wife. Or my *bruder*."

At her stiff nod, he pivoted and headed with relief toward the gathering. Ben made the walk back at a slower pace than when he'd come out. He was grateful it was a bit of a distance, as he had much to think about. He still didn't know what he was going to do about his marriage. Or the rumors he believed had truth to them. But at least now, they'd hopefully just be his and Rachel's business to deal with, and no one else's.

The rest of the afternoon, until he noticed subtle signs that Rachel was getting tired and needed to get off her feet, he kept a wary eye on where Lydia was and what she was doing. The redheaded woman kept her mouth mainly closed. Her gaze slanted to him a few times, more in the manner she was aware he was watching than that she was saying something she shouldn't.

When Rachel idly asked whcre he'd gone during their ride home, Ben just shook his head. "Had some… bad apples that needed addressing."

The ribbons of Rachel's *kapp* danced about her chin as she cocked her head to consider him. "At the picnic? That's odd. But always good to sort them out as soon as possible, I guess. They can spoil quite a few surrounding ones if you wait too long."

"That's what I figured." Their marriage had enough internal challenges without outside rumors and opinions weighing on it.

He could see Rachel's profile from the corner of his eye. Was she ever planning to tell him? Ben noticed his knee bouncing as his foot kept tapping on the floor of thc buggy. To still the restless movement, he crossed the other foot over his ankle. Did it matter whether she told him or not? It might take a while to sort out his feelings, but the knowledge wouldn't have changed his actions.

What would Aaron think if he came back and found his brother raising his child? His fingers tightened on the reins, causing Sojourner to toss her head and jangle the bridle. Relaxing his hands, Ben reminded himself it didn't matter who'd fathered the babe.

Still, he wanted to know.

Chapter Eight

"**I**'m nervous." Rachel's apron was wadded in her hands.

"I suppose that's normal." Ben rubbed his own sweaty palms together as, looking out the window, he watched the Mennonite midwife who served the district drive her car up the lane.

"I'm glad you suggested it was time to contact Mrs. Edigers. I didn't know how long I should wait before we did. Some women wait longer when they are with child." Dropping the apron, Rachel rested a hand on her stomach. "But maybe not with their first?"

She was chattering. Rachel never chattered. Was she worried about what the midwife's visit might reveal? She was also looking at him like she thought he had answers. He certainly didn't. But he wanted to. It wouldn't change the way he felt about Rachel. Or the coming baby. But he wanted to know. Was this baby coming much sooner than they'd thought? Correction, than he thought? He glanced at Rachel's anxious yet excited face as she watched the Mennonite woman and Hannah Bartel, an Amish woman now apprenticing with her, get out of the car. Would Rachel do that to him, knowing he would raise the child as his own, regardless of whether he was the father, or…the uncle?

Ach, hopefully they would soon know. Forcing down a swallow, he strode to the door to open it to the two women and their armloads of equipment.

Over the next fifteen minutes, Ben slowly paced the house as Mrs. Edigers asked Rachel questions regarding family history, her own health history, what she'd been eating and how she'd been feeling amongst other things while Hannah took his wife's pulse and blood pressure. He turned his back but remained hovering at the door when Rachel lay down on the bed.

"Now what does that do?" he heard her ask.

"We're listening for the baby's heartbeat," was the midwife's calm answer.

Ben straightened from where he'd been leaning against the doorframe. A heartbeat? The thought of a separate heartbeat made the child so much more real. He twisted so he could see the trio at the bed. Mrs. Edigers had the device on Rachel's stomach, her eyes narrowed as she listened intently. When he saw the midwife's eyes widen, he turned fully, stiffening as he watched her shift the device to different areas of Rachel's exposed stomach. Was everything all right? He fisted his hands. *A boppeli* or *your boppeli* didn't matter at all as long as Rachel and the babe were all right. Please, *Gott*, let them be all right.

Ben released the breath he hadn't been aware he was holding in a loud exhale when the older woman's face softened into a smile. Glancing in his direction, she winked. Ben jerked his head back. What did that mean? Had she sensed his concern and was advising him everything was okay?

The Mennonite woman straightened. Handing the device to Hannah, she nodded toward where she'd been listening. With a perplexed expression, Hannah bent over Rachel's midsection. After a few moments, her eyes widened, as well. Ben was two steps farther into the room before he realized he was moving.

Mrs. Edigers helped shift his wife so she rested with her back against the headboard. "Rachel, good thing you're sitting down. Maybe you want to as well, Ben. I have some big news for you." The older woman chuckled as she patted Rachel's shoulder. "I heard not one heartbeat, but two. You're having twins."

Rachel gasped as her round-eyed gaze swiveled to Ben. "Twins? Two *boppeli*?"

Ben dazedly figured her dropped jaw and stunned expression mirrored his. "Are you joking?"

Mrs. Edigers's smile expanded. "Yes, two babies. No, no joke. I imagine you've been quite tired. That would also explain why you're a bit bigger than you might have expected. From your measurements and what you've indicated, they should arrive sometime early October, as multiple babies usually come a few weeks earlier than a single pregnancy."

Everything else the midwife was saying was lost in the buzzing in Ben's ears. Two babies? They were going to have two babies? His heart was racing. He staggered out of the room to sink into his cushioned chair. Arriving in early October? That meant... Ben's ears reddened. Twins in October meant he should never have doubted his wife. His fingers curled over the smooth oak arms of his chair. It didn't matter. It wouldn't have mattered. He would be husband to Rachel and father to the child regardless. But now, he'd be father to two. And they were his. Not his brother's. Ben slumped with simple joy and relief at the thought. Two babies at once? His head flopped back on the chair. He didn't know how to be a father to one.

Hopefully *Gott* knew what He was doing, as Ben certainly didn't.

"How are you doing, new *daed*?" Still dazed ten minutes later, he hadn't heard Hannah Bartel enter the room.

Blinking to clear his vision and rein in his galloping thoughts, Ben saw her smiling down at him. "I don't know yet. It will take a while to sink in. I was still getting used to one *boppeli*. And now to have two?" He'd seen multiplies before with sheep and cattle. He'd remembered in the last few moments there were other twins in the district, but he'd never thought he'd belong in that group. His bemused grin ebbed and his brow lowered as he tried to recall any issues those with twins had experienced. Sometimes twin calves didn't thrive. He sat up abruptly. "What does carrying two *boppeli* do to the mother? Will two *boppeli* be all right?"

"I don't know enough at this time to give you advice on either of those questions. This is my first set of twins. But I'll learn and I'll let you know. I'm sure the *boppeli* will be smaller than a single birth. As for how it affects the mother?" Hannah shook her head. "I just don't know yet."

Pushing to his feet, Ben nodded vaguely. Surely Mrs. Edigers had some answers, but, whereas he'd grown up with Hannah and might discuss the topic with her, he didn't know the midwife well enough to feel comfortable yet asking these questions. Peeking through the door to his wife's bedroom, he saw her cradle her rounded belly in wonder. The ends of Ben's lips tipped up at the sight. He would find out the information though. He'd do whatever was needed to take care of his family. It's what he did.

"Maybe you should sit down. Can I get you anything?"

Rachel, standing at the sink, looked over to where Ben came in the door from doing the evening cattle chores. This was the first he'd had a chance to speak to her after their big—he raised his eyebrows at the understatement—news. He'd waved from the barn when Mrs. Edigers and Hannah left. The livestock had needed tending and he'd had too much nervous energy with the afternoon's shocking revelation to stay put in the house.

Her smile still held more than a hint of wonder. "Physically, I feel no different than when I woke up this morning. But mentally?" Rachel shook her head. "I can't wrap my mind around it." She accepted Ben's hand as he led her to sit in a chair by the table.

"Well, that explains why you are…" With his hands, Ben vaguely shaped around his stomach.

"As big as some of the milk cows on Zook's farm?" Rachel offered helpfully.

Ben grinned as he sat across from her, "*Nee*. But maybe bigger than other women with child are at this stage." Rachel eyed him quizzically. His smile drooping, Ben rubbed the back of his neck. "Not that I go around looking at women who might be…" Squirming, he brought his hand around to rub over his mouth and looked down, finishing in a mutter, "But you seemed bigger. And I thought…"

When he raised his head, Rachel regarded him with a frown. "You thought…" Then her eyes widened. "You thought it was Aaron's baby," she whispered.

Ben simply nodded. He wished to look anywhere except at her, but he knew it would be cowardly so he kept his gaze on her stark expression.

"I would never do that to you." Her eyes were dark with hurt.

Ben wanted to reach for her. Instead, inhaling raggedly, he clasped his hands together and hid them under the table. "I… It wouldn't have made any difference. I still would've married you. Regardless. I would have loved the child as my own. No difference."

"I never… He and I never…"

Ben's gut clenched at the tears welling in her brown depths, making her beautiful eyes glisten.

"I can't believe you thought that of me." Rachel's voice trembled as much as her lower lip.

He couldn't stand it. Ben reached out a hand toward her, for what purpose, he didn't know. It didn't matter anyway. Ignoring it and him, Rachel pushed to her feet and returned to the sink.

"Supper will be on the table in a few minutes if you want to take the time to wash up." She didn't turn. Her posture was as stiff as her voice.

With a slumped head, Ben rose from his chair and trudged to the bathroom. What he wanted to wash was his mouth out with soap. Why hadn't he just stayed quiet about his concerns? Either way, they wouldn't have made any difference. Was it because he was just so elated to have that concern lifted? To know he really hadn't been used, just because he was available and had a habit of cleaning up after his brother? It wouldn't have mattered. His actions would've been the same. Still, as he'd reminded himself earlier, it was better to be silent and appear a fool than to speak and remove all doubt. Look where this acknowledgement had gotten him.

Now his wife was distressed. Ben turned on the water at the sink, washed his hands and splashed water on the back of his neck. Glancing in the small mirror above the sink that he used when shaving, Ben fingered the beard that marked him as a married man as he frowned at his reflection. He knew Rachel's character from way back. Deceit wasn't in her nature. He should've trusted *Gott* and trusted his wife. Shaking his head at his reflection, he thought back over the afternoon.

Twins! He hadn't fully grasped the concept of one *boppeli* yet.

A gasp and crash from the kitchen had him bouncing off the doorjamb as he dashed from the bathroom. Hurrying across the room, he took in the plate on the floor and the sight of his wife, one hand braced on the counter and the other touching her rounded apron.

Avoiding the broken plate, Ben skidded to a halt before her. "Are you all right!"

She turned toward him with a dazed expression. "I think so."

"What happened?" Ben bent to pick up the pieces of the broken plate and carry them to the trash.

"I think I felt…" Rachel's cheeks and the shell of her ears, exposed by her *kapp*, were a charming pink. "I think I felt the *boppeli* move."

Taking a step back, Ben braced his hip on the table. He needed the support of four legs as his two were unsteady. "Are you sure?"

"I'm not too sure of anything right now, but I've never felt anything like it before. According to Mrs. Edigers, I should be able to feel them soon." She gave a breathless giggle. "I guess this is soon."

Ben sagged more heavily against the table, gazing in amazement at his wife's midsection. First a heartbeat, and now movement. The vague concept that'd prompted their marriage was becoming real at the speed of stampeding cattle. Lifting a hand toward her, he instantly jerked it back. Crossing his arms, he tucked his palms into his armpits to keep from touching her.

Rachel didn't seem to notice. "I don't feel it on the outside. Only on the—" if possible, her cheeks turned even more crimson "—inside. It's a sort of fluttering. Like a butterfly." She shook her head. "Two. Oh, my…" Astonishment faded to be replaced by the dawning of concern. "The midwife said they'd be smaller than a single baby. I hope they're all right."

"I know. But whatever happens is *Gott*'s will." Even as he said the words, Ben couldn't help hoping it be *Gott*'s will that the two, becoming more real and so precious to him, would be safe and healthy, even if he didn't know what to do with them once they arrived. But one thing he knew he should and could do, was make it right with their mother.

"I'm sorry, Rachel. I should never have thought…" Ben's shoulders lifted in a guilty sigh "…what I did. I should've known you'd never do something like that. I'm sorry I ever doubted you."

With a glance at a few plate chips remaining on the

linoleum floor, she carefully stepped around him to get the broom and dustpan from the closet. Dropping his arms and straightening from the table, Ben took the dustpan from her to squat down and place it next to the plate pieces on the floor. When the broom didn't move, he looked up to see a rueful twist on Rachel's lips.

"Was it because of the rumors?"

He couldn't prevent a wince. "You heard about those?"

The broom went into brisk motion. "I think that was the intention."

After the last whisks into the dustpan, he rose and dumped the contents in the trash. He met Rachel at the closet door. Reaching out, she grabbed the edge of the dustpan and held it between them until she had his full attention.

"*Denki.* And you're forgiven." She put the tool away and shut the closet door. "I know Plain people don't generally speak about a woman with child. That doesn't mean some aren't thinking and watching. And given my size, you probably aren't the only one to think what you did."

Still whirling with relief at her first words, Ben almost didn't hear her last ones. When he didn't speak, Rachel grimaced. "I'm sorry on that, as it affects you, as well."

He shook his head. "I can handle myself." Recalling his conversation with Lydia, a slow smile slid over his face. "And I don't think that person will be saying anything more." As for him, he wouldn't doubt his wife again. "What do you want to do now? Let this news trickle into community knowledge? Or let them continue to wonder?"

Rachel grinned impishly. "I'm tempted to let them continue to wonder." Her expression faded a bit as she continued, "But if they've heard the rumors, I don't want to do that to my family or yours. Besides," her bright smile returned, "I can't wait to let my *mamm* know she'll be a *grossmammi* to two."

"I wouldn't mind telling my folks the news, as well. We'll let things go from there as they will then." Although he longed to do more, Ben limited himself to taking one of her delicate, deceptively strong hands in his. "And Rachel, one, two or ten *boppeli*, I know you'll make a *wunderbar* mother."

She blushed, her hand momentarily tightening on his. "*Gut* thing I helped care for my younger *schweschder* and little *bruder* when I was growing up."

"You have the advantage over me. I have far more younger siblings than you, but I have to admit, when they squalled or smelled, I'd race out of the house to the barn, leaving Sarah to help *Mamm* while I shadowed *Daed* and—" Ben caught himself before he said Aaron's name. His gut clenched as he cleared his throat. "And learned what to do in the barn and fields." He forced a grin. "If there's anything with the *boppeli* that requires a pitchfork or feed bucket, make sure you let me know."

"I think with two, you'll be called upon to learn a few new things."

"With two," Ben echoed, shaking his head. His smile became natural. "Oh, help."

Rachel nodded understandingly at the common Amish phrase. "Oh, help indeed."

Sharing a warm gaze that jolted Ben almost as much as news of the twins, they slowly released their clasped hands. Rachel turned to the cupboard to get a plate to replace the broken one. Ben sat in his chair and eyed the contents on the table. The potatoes were no longer steaming. The gravy looked a bit congealed. The dressing had slid off the cucumbers. But to Ben, it seemed like the best meal he'd had in a long, long time. It was the first one where it finally seemed there was just him and Rachel in the marriage, without his brother's shadow hanging over them.

Chapter Nine

Rachel glanced out the kitchen window at the clatter of hooves coming up the lane. She smiled when she recognized her sister Rebecca's rig. Rinsing the quart jar she'd just washed, she set it upside down on the rack to dry and shook the water off her hands. Grabbing a dish towel, she finished wiping them as she walked to the door. Rachel's smile dimmed at the expression on her sister's face as Rebecca hurried up the steps.

"Is everything all right? Is *Mamm* okay? And Amos?"

"*Ja, ja.* I'm sorry, I didn't mean to make you worry." Rebecca gave her a quick hug as she came through the door. When Rachel closed it behind her and followed her into the kitchen, Rebecca withdrew an envelope from the waistband of her apron.

"This came for you at home. I wasn't sure what you wanted to do with it. Or whom you might want to see it. So I brought it right over."

Brows furrowed, Rachel took the long white envelope from her sister's outstretched hand. She stiffened as her fingers pinched the slender missive. Although there was no return address, Rachel recognized the handwriting that scrawled her maiden name and previous address across the front of the envelope. He'd written her before a few times while they'd been walking out. Why would Aaron send her a letter now, after all this time?

She looked up to find Rebecca watching her expectantly. With a tight smile, Rachel shook her head. "I'll read it later." She tucked it into the waistband of her own apron. Her sister's expression briefly revealed her disappointment but she nodded understandably.

"*Denki* for bringing it over. I have no idea what it might say, but you're right. Until I do, it's probably best that no one knows he sent it."

Intentionally changing the subject, she walked with Rebecca out into the garden and picked a few summer squash to send home. Although she greatly enjoyed her sister's visits, today the minutes weighed as heavy as the letter tucked into her waistband until the younger woman indicated it was time for her to go. Upon waving goodbye as Rebecca drove down the lane, Rachel returned to the house. With damp palms, she retrieved the envelope and stared at it.

Why now? She'd almost forgotten him. Her life was so full with just learning about the two babies a week ago and… Ben. A twinge of guilt flickered over her face. She could barely remember what Aaron looked like and she'd intended to marry the man for years. He was dark-haired and blue-eyed like his brother, but whenever she tried to visualize his face, instead of a square jaw, she saw a cheek that dimpled with a rare shy smile. Rachel tapped the letter against her palm. What could it possibly say?

There was one way to find out.

With a sharp inhale, she slid a finger into the edge and tore the flap open, the crackle of the ripping envelope causing a small shudder to run up her spine. Pulling out the single sheet of paper, Rachel unfolded it and quickly scanned the contents.

Dear Rachel, I've been thinking of you. I didn't intend to hurt you. I do care for you. Aaron.

She stared at the simple pen strokes, the words becoming blurry as the backs of her eyes prickled with tears. That was it? And after all this time, what did it mean? One tear dripped, dampening the paper as memories of the relationship that'd meant everything to her during her *rumspringa* flooded through her. Memories of the man whose sweet words had made her feel special. Whom she'd thought was *Gott*'s chosen one for her. Why did Aaron have to send this now, when things had been going well between her and Ben? With one last look at the brief words, she refolded the letter and slid it back into the envelope.

Any way she could think of it, this would not help her relationship with her husband. There was no news about his brother she could pass on to Ben. It didn't say where Aaron was, why he left, or when or even if he was coming back. Only that he was thinking of and cared for her. The envelope crinkled as her hand tightened around it. Her. Who was now his brother's wife. Did Aaron know that? Opening her hand, she ran her thumb over the address. Obviously not, as he'd addressed it to her maiden name.

Smoothing out the wrinkles she'd created, Rachel gazed at the wastepaper basket. If there'd been something in it to share with Ben, she would have. As it was, there was no reason to keep the missive. Still—she pressed the letter to her chest—she couldn't let it go. When she'd moved out of her old home, she'd thrown all mementos of her relationship with Aaron in a tearful purging. This was the only thing from him she had now. Although troubling, it brought back memories, good ones, of a carefree girl romanced by a charming fellow. Instead of being a new wife in a tenuous marriage, heavy with child and the responsibilities of running a household. Could she ever totally let go of that carefree girl?

Rachel tapped the envelope against her side a moment before she crossed to her bedroom and opened the drawer of the nightstand next to her bed. Dropping the envelope in, she shut the drawer again with a rueful sigh. *Oh, Aaron. You did hurt me. Everything has changed because you left. And can't return to what it was. If you return to confront the repercussions of your abrupt departure, there'll be more of us hurt. Maybe it's best if you stay away.* Her heart clenched at the thought. She reached for the drawer again, only to curl her fingers into a fist before opening it. With a resolve to dispose of the letter at some point—just not yet—Rachel returned to the kitchen to continue preparations for the day's canning.

When Ben asked that evening about her day, she told him about the canning and her sister's visit, and nothing else.

Waving a casual farewell to coworkers still harnessing their horses after work, Ben guided Sojy down Main Street, his thoughts already turning toward Rachel. He snorted with self-derision. He was always

thinking of Rachel. But now, amongst the silent longing and muted joy was a tinge of worry. She'd been
quiet the past few days. Rachel wasn't a loquacious
woman anyway, and he knew she was often tired when
he got into the house after work and chores at the end
of the day, but the past couple days since she'd mentioned Rebecca had visited, his wife had been excep-
tionally subdued.

Had Rebecca brought bad news? Ben sighed, sick
at heart that he and his wife still didn't have the relationship where they could talk easily together. Surely
she would've told him if something was wrong at her
mamm's farm? Had Rachel and her *schweschder* ar-
gued? Ben didn't want to get into the middle of two
sisters bickering, but, his lips flattened grimly as
he passed The Dew Drop restaurant where Rebecca
worked, he'd do whatever was necessary to protect his
wife. Whether or not she was growing more burdened
by day with carrying his two children.

Maybe that was the reason. Maybe she was even
more fatigued, as there were two *boppeli* instead of
one. Rachel never complained, but he'd detected winces
and grimaces crossing her face when she didn't think
he was watching. Was she worried now that they knew
there were two? Did she know something about multiples that he didn't? Pregnancy and childbirth were very
normal in the Amish community, as they welcomed
and rejoiced in large families. That didn't mean there
weren't occasional problems. In fact, their neighbor
Jethro Weaver had lost his wife and unborn child last
fall due to a pregnancy-related issue.

After they'd been advised of the twins, Ben had
noted all the twins existing around the district. Although

somewhat rare, there were a few. Did carrying twins bring increased risks for the mother? His stomach began to churn at the thought of losing his wife and children like Jethro had. Was there something Rachel wasn't telling him that had her silent with worry?

He was approaching the cheerfully colored awning of the quilt shop where Hannah Bartel, the apprentice to the midwife, still occasionally worked. Slowing his horse, Ben peered into the windows of The Stitch. To his relief, he saw Hannah inside. Before he could talk himself out of it, he guided a surprised Sojourner to the curb. Hopping out, Ben secured the mare and headed for the shop door, his step slowing when he noted other shoppers were inside.

Pausing outside the door, he debated his hasty decision. He knew all the women visible in the shop, but still, he didn't want them to hear his questions for Hannah. Drumming his fingers on his thigh, he weighed his and Rachel's privacy against settling his concerns regarding her and the *boppeli*. He glanced at the shop hours stenciled on the door's window before narrowing his eyes at the clock visible inside on an interior wall. A few moments until closing time. Hopefully the women would soon finish their business and leave. Ben shifted his feet when he saw that he'd drawn their curious attention. Heaving a sigh, he pushed open the door and stepped inside.

The three women at the counter smiled as he stepped inside. His boss's wife, Ruth Schrock, called out the first greeting.

"*Guder Nummidaag*, Ben." Although her expression remained bland, he recognized the impishness in her eyes. "When did you start quilting?" Having grown up with Ruth and worked with her at Fisher Furniture when her *daed* owned the shop before Malachi bought it, Ben wasn't surprised at her teasing.

"Good afternoon to you, as well. And this is nothing new—you always have me in stitches." The trio of women giggled at his response. He strolled toward them through the rows of fabric. Might as well brazen it out now. "She's grown." He nodded to Deborah, the baby girl, dressed just like her *mamm*, who peered curiously at him from the safety of Ruth's arms. He swallowed hard at the thought, the hope, that one like her would be nestled in Rachel's arms sometime in the future.

"She certainly has. It's a race between Deborah and Rascal as to who can scurry over the floor faster now."

Ben nodded to Ruth's companion, another woman he'd grown up with. He'd been glad when Hannah's *schweschder*, Gail Lapp, now Gail Schrock as she'd married Malachi's *bruder* Samuel, had returned to the community with her young daughter. "And how are you, Lily?" He nodded toward the little blond girl currently petting Socks, Hannah's Border collie and frequent companion.

Eyeing him warily, the girl gave the dog a few more strokes before solemnly stating, *"Ich bin gut."* She glanced up at her *mamm*. "I said that right, didn't I?"

Rubbing a hand over his mouth, Ben hid a smile. Whereas most Amish children spoke the Pennsylvania Dutch dialect at home and didn't learn English until they attended school, Lily had it backward, having lived in the *Englisch* world for the first few years of her life and only returning with Gail to Miller's Creek last summer. Lily tugged on her *mamm*'s apron. "Can we go home? I want to watch *Daed* work with the filly."

Ben's grin behind his hand grew larger. Samuel Schrock, also a previous coworker before he'd become the horse trader for the community, was going to have his hands full with this *maedel*. Ben couldn't wish it on a better man. And nothing would be said, but as was evident by Gail's profile when her apron had been tugged, Samuel was also going to be a *daed* again at some point. Ben was thrilled for his friend.

But now he wanted to ask the midwife apprentice about his own wife's condition. Hannah met his eyes and smiled in understanding. She turned her attention to the little girl. "I think you're going to have a lovely new dress with that material, Lily. Will you be wearing it next church Sunday?"

Gail Schrock picked up a bag from the counter. "I don't know if it'll be done by then, because I'll have to get someone to stand still long enough to take measurements before I can make it. Come on, Lily, let's go see how the filly's training is coming." With a wave of farewell, she followed her skipping daughter to the door.

When the little girl departed, Socks trotted to the dog bed in the corner and settled on it. Ben watched as she stretched out her black-and-white legs and rested her head upon them.

"Where's Nip and Tuck?" Hannah and her husband, Gabe, had rescued the two Border collie pups during one of Gabe's EMS calls this past winter.

Hannah shook her head with a smile. "They're out at my folks' farm until we can get a bigger place. The apartment upstairs was getting a little too small for all of us."

Ruth snagged a small bag from the counter. "We need to be heading out as well as we're riding home with Malachi. We're supposed to meet him at the shop after work. As you're here, he may be ready to go, as well." She squinted at Ben. "Although I'm still trying to figure out why you are here."

"You keep thinking on that. It should entertain you for a while."

She flashed him a smile, but after studying his face for a moment, Ruth's expression grew more serious. "It's *gut* to see you joking again, Ben. We've been worried about you."

"Ach," Ben ducked his head as his cheeks reddened. "I'm fine. I'll always be fine."

"Gut to know." Ruth reached out to briefly touch his arm before she shifted the girl in her arms, bid him and Hannah farewell and left the shop.

"I'm guessing you're here because you're worried about someone else. I'm also guessing from what she said, you haven't shared the news about the twins."

"Only to our parents, because of the…" he scowled "…rumors. Everyone else will just have to find out when they arrive."

Hannah frowned, as well. "When they come early, as multiples frequently do, some might not know that. They'll count the months and still wonder."

"Those that want to will do that. I can't change what they think. They're not my business. Rachel is. What have you learned?" He prompted the apprentice midwife.

He wasn't encouraged when, frowning further, she sighed. "Well, there are greater risks for complication

FREE BOOKS GIVEAWAY

ET UP TO FOUR FREE BOOKS
& TWO FREE GIFTS
WORTH OVER $20!

We pay for everything!

YOU pick your books – WE pay for everything.

You get up to FOUR New Books and TWO Mystery Gifts...absolutely FRE

Dear Reader,

I am writing to announce the launch of a huge **FREE BOOK GIVEAWAY**... and to let you know that YOU are entitled to choose up to FOUR fantastic books that WE pay for.

Try **Love Inspired® Romance Larger-Print** books and fall in love with inspirational romances that take you on an uplifting journey of faith, forgiveness and hope.

Try **Love Inspired® Suspense Larger-Print** books where courage and optimism unite in stories of faith and love in the face of danger.

Or TRY BOTH!

In return, we ask just one favor: Would you please participate in our brief Reader Survey? We'd love to hear from you.

This FREE BOOKS GIVEAWAY means that we pay for *everything!* We'll even cover the shipping, and no purchas is necessary, now or later. So please return your survey today. You'll get **Two Free Books** and **Two Mystery Gifts** from each series to try, altogether worth over **$20!**

Sincerely

Pam Powers

Pam Powers
For Harlequin Reader Servi

Complete the survey below and return it today to receive up to 4 FREE BOOKS and FREE GIFTS guaranteed!

FREE BOOKS GIVEAWAY
Reader Survey

1

Do you prefer books which reflect Christian values?

◯ YES ◯ NO

2

Do you share your favorite books with friends?

◯ YES ◯ NO

3

Do you often choose to read instead of watching TV?

◯ YES ◯ NO

YES! Please send me my Free Rewards, consisting of **2 Free Books from each series I select** and **Free Mystery Gifts**. I understand that I am under no obligation to buy anything, as explained on the back of this card.

❑ **Love Inspired® Romance Larger-Print** (122/322 IDL GQ36)
❑ **Love Inspired® Suspense Larger-Print** (107/307 IDL GQ36)
❑ **Try Both** (122/322 & 107/307 IDL GQ4J)

FIRST NAME ____ LAST NAME ____

ADDRESS ____

APT.# ____ CITY ____

STATE/PROV. ____ ZIP/POSTAL CODE ____

EMAIL ❑ Please check this box if you would like to receive newsletters and promotional emails from Harlequin Enterprises ULC and its affiliates. You can unsubscribe anytime.

with twins. Although that doesn't mean they'll happen," she hastened to assure him.

"Like what?"

"With the *boppeli* in all likelihood arriving early, it means they'll have low birth weights." She met his somber gaze. "Along with corresponding issues."

Ben grew up with livestock. He knew about runts and their struggle to thrive. He pivoted to stare blindly at the far wall, the bright-colored quilts that adorned it counter to his bleak thoughts. Amish districts differed. Some tended to reject extraordinary measures to save a life, since such measures may attempt to interfere with *Gott*'s will. As Amish carried no health insurance, relying on the church and community to cover member's incurred bills, expenses born by his family would affect the whole district. What were they to do if the babes were born too small to survive? Would *Gott* punish him through his children for his sin of being in love with his brother's intended? For stealing her for himself? Ben's head lowered as his eyes closed. With hands pressed to his chest, he emptied his mind and opened his heart. *Gott, please forgive me. It is my sin, and my sin alone. I am in awe that You've brought Rachel and these children into my life. Please forgive me of this sin against my brother.*

With a shuddering sigh, Ben opened his eyes and lifted his head. A good part of the *boppeli* staying healthy depended on the health of his wife.

"What about for Rachel?" He directed the question over his shoulder.

Hannah hesitated before continuing softly. "Some frequent issues of women carrying twins are higher risk for gestational diabetes, anemia and preeclampsia."

Ben hissed in his breath. Eclampsia had been determined as the cause of death for Jethro's wife and child.

"More morning sickness."

"*Ach*, she's certainly had that." He turned to face Hannah.

"I'd always heard so, but having now seen her numerous times in action, I can vouch for the fact that Mrs. Edigers is very *gut* at what she does. She'll take *gut* care of them."

"As I'm sure that you'll be as talented as well, by the time you finish your apprenticeship." He smiled ruefully.

"I hope so. I'll certainly strive to be."

"Well, I should be going. I have chores and Rachel will be expecting me. *Denki* for the information, Hannah. I can't say it's comforting to know, but I'd rather know than be ignorant. Tell Gabe hello for me." He turned and began weaving his way back through the brightly colored rows.

"Will do and we'll keep a close eye on any issues with Rachel and the *boppeli*. It might be difficult convincing her, but as she gets closer to their arrival, it would help her to get off her feet. *Sehn dich scheeder*, Ben."

"*Ja*. See you later," he echoed, the bell above the door jangling as he exited.

Ben's brow remained furrowed as the familiar countryside breezed by during the drive home. He had to take care of his wife. Always his intention, the need pulsed through him with this new information. How to do so? If he didn't know she'd already have supper on the table, he would've returned to The Dew Drop to take something home for them. He blinked and shifted on the seat. Why hadn't he thought of that before? He'd tell Rachel he'd pick something up for them tomorrow so she wouldn't have to cook.

How else could he care for her? There were a few hours of daylight after supper. He could go to the garden instead of reading the paper and do the hoeing so Rachel didn't have to.

Ben's customary glance toward the kitchen window as he drove up the lane turned worried when Rachel didn't appear there to wave. With a frown, he scanned the garden. She wasn't there either. Directing Sojy to the barn, he left her in front of its big door as he hurried toward the house.

It was quiet when he entered. "Rachel?" he called softly. The kitchen was empty, albeit the table was set for two. A garden salad sat on the counter. A steaming casserole was visible in the oven, although the appliance was off, its door open a crack.

He found her in her rocking chair. Ben's air was stranded in his throat, until he saw the steady rise and fall of her breathing. She'd fallen asleep. She'd spared a moment during the day to sit down and had fallen asleep. Her hands rested across her midsection. Her head was tipped to one side against the back of the rocker. A few strands of dark hair had fallen from under her still neatly pinned *kapp* to drape across her cheek. Her eyelashes fanned over the dark circles under her eyes.

For a moment, Ben just watched her sleep. For years, he'd never been able to look his fill at Rachel. First, it would've drawn teasing from his fellow schoolmates if they'd caught him watching one of the girls. Then, when she was Aaron's, it hadn't seemed right. After he and Rachel were married, the way their relationship had begun, and stood, he knew it would make her uncomfortable to gaze at her as he wanted to.

When she didn't stir, he gingerly unpinned her *kapp* and took it with him into her bedroom. Setting it on the nightstand by the bed, he turned down the handmade quilt and cotton sheet. Returning to the rocker, Ben gazed down at her again with a soft smile on his face. Rachel hadn't been sleeping well. He could hear her moving around when he wasn't sleeping. He longed to guard her rest, because when the babes came, from what he'd heard, neither of them would get much sleep at first. She was always working. Even though she was tired, she never complained.

Bending down, Ben gently curled his arms about her and lifted her from the chair. Her head lolled against his neck. Ducking his chin, Ben tenderly kissed her forehead. Resting his head against hers, his eyes drifted closed as longing to be able to do that freely rippled through him. With a regretful sigh, he carried Rachel into her bedroom and carefully laid her down on the bed. Conscious of the day's warmth, he pulled the sheet only over her, tucking it at her shoulders.

"I know I'm not the one you want to hear it from. I shouldn't say it. But I can't hold the words back. You're beautiful. I don't understand why *Gott* saw fit to make you mine. But I'm so thankful He did. And I'll do everything in my power that someday, hopefully, you'll be thankful, as well."

He froze as she murmured something and shifted to her side. When she resettled, he placed one last kiss on the coiled length of her hair and quietly left the room.

Chapter Ten

Ben leaned the bag of feed against the wall, grabbed the tab at the top and jerked it open with a resulting *brr* sound as the heavy thread ripped loose from the reinforced paper. As he poured the brown pellets into two pails, his thoughts were far away from his task.

His earliest memories regarding chores on the farm had been of tailing after his older *bruder*. Aaron had been the one to show him how to carefully maneuver about in the corn bin. He'd been the one to show him how to harness their pony. Aaron had taught him how to tie his first boots when it'd gotten too cold in the fall to go barefoot. How to put a worm on a hook, how to take a fish off and how to get one on in between. Ben had been two steps behind the older *bruder* he'd adored all the time when they were young. Their folks had even commented on it, joking, Gut *thing we named them with the first letters of A and B, as Benjamin's always following Aaron.*

Unhooking the barn door, Ben slipped through carrying the first two pails of corn he'd filled earlier. "Hey, back off," he admonished the numerous black-

and-white heads crowding around him. "You'll all be fed soon if you're just a little patient. Just let me get through." Bumping the buckets against some noses that got a little too close, he made his way through the restless steers to the feed bunks. Ben grimaced as he noted the end bunk he'd destroyed weeks earlier to save the steer. *I need to get that fixed. Always something to do, particularly with livestock.* Pouring the two buckets in a long line down one of the other two bunks, he hurried back to the barn for two more pails of corn. The cattle, except for a few, were jostling for position at the first bunk, freeing his path to the second.

He glanced over to where Rachel was working in the garden. Although breakfast had been more leisurely this morning as he didn't have to go to town for work, they still hadn't talked much. She'd been charmingly disconcerted and apologetic about falling asleep before supper last night. And about finding the kitchen cleaned up when she'd awakened this morning.

Enjoying her rosy cheeks, he'd assured her it was fine. And it had been. More than fine. He'd treasure those quiet moments for some time, never knowing when he'd have a chance to store up more.

Emptying the buckets, Ben returned to the barn, his gaze still on Rachel in the garden. The first time he'd wondered about gardening was when his *grossmammi* had called him and Aaron two peas in a pod. That's the way they'd remained growing up. At home, at church, at school, where Ben had expressed little interest because he was shy and much more intrigued with any other aspects of life. But anything Aaron could do—except for schoolwork—Ben strove to emulate his hero older brother.

For sure and certain, they'd been competitive. They'd played baseball on opposite teams, raced horses, competed eating the most pancakes and throwing hay bales the farthest. But he and Aaron had been best friends, even though his older *bruder* seemed to always have been a little better, a little faster, a little smarter.

Until Aaron entered his *rumspringa*.

Then everything changed. Ben was left behind as Aaron's close friends became the ones he met at the parties he was either attending or continuously talking about. With those, and other *Englisch* pursuits as his main interests, he was frequently distracted from his work on the farm. Then it was Ben that came along, finishing up tasks or correcting errors so Aaron didn't get into trouble when he'd head out early to meet up with guys driving cars to parties. A cell phone and charger were tucked into the dresser the two shared, along with magazines on mechanics and *Englisch* blue jeans. Aaron no longer sported a bowl cut, his hair was now trimmed shorter under a ball cap instead of a straw or felt hat.

The only Amish thing Aaron seemed to enjoy was courting Rachel. When Ben finally entered his *rumspringa*, his *bruder* had already paired off with the girl he'd always admired. Although he was glad to spend time with his Amish friends, the only reason Ben had gone to singings and *youngie* parties was to see Rachel. And torture himself that she was now with Aaron.

Nudging the barn door open with his shoulder, Ben carried out the two pails of pellets. He'd been shocked Aaron had left Rachel. But even though they'd taken baptism classes together, although he'd been disappointed and heartsick at Aaron's disappearance, Ben wasn't really that surprised his *bruder* had left for the *Englisch* life he'd seemed so fascinated with. As Ben climbed into the first bunk to walk between the cattle's broad heads and sprinkle the pellets on top of the rapidly disappearing corn, he wondered what Aaron would've come up with to delay baptism into the church if he hadn't been kicked by the horse and broken his arm that Sunday morning. Aaron had left without being baptized. He could therefore return to the community without severe consequences. Had that been his plan all along? If he'd left after having been baptized, he'd have been shunned if he came back. The fact that he hadn't been baptized left the door open for a return. The now empty pails banging against his legs, Ben glanced again at his wife's profile as he climbed down from the bunk.

Ach, maybe Aaron's consequences of departure, if he planned to return, had been rather severe after all.

Rachel straightened and arched her back before resting a hand on the underside of her burgeoning middle. As this was mid-July and the midwife had mentioned early October, she couldn't imagine how she'd be able to work closer to when the *boppeli* would arrive. While she was still wrapping her mind around the thought of two, her body well knew the burden she carried.

Heaving a sigh, she considered the wall of vines climbing up the woven wire ahead. She appreciated Ben's idea of the fence for the cucumbers more than he'd know. Gathering her apron into a basket, she dropped the summer squash into it and trudged toward the end of the garden, curling her bare toes into the sun-warmed tilled earth. Rachel relished in the sensation, but when she recognized the beginning of a waddle in her gait, she winced.

Her face warmed as she recalled that she'd slept while Ben had taken care of her and the supper chores. Although she appreciated his constant solicitousness, it always seemed directed toward her as a woman with child. *Ach*, Rachel sighed, it would be hard to see a woman who walked like a duck as anything but that at the moment.

She wanted to be seen as a woman who was attractive to her husband. But it understandably would be hard for him to see her that way when the whole of their marriage, she'd been a swirling mess of emotions and physical changes. Surely a man didn't find his wife attractive when she was red-eyed with weeping, or wearing a deathly pallor as she raced for the bathroom. Or looking like she'd swallowed a watermelon whole instead of tending to its vines.

At least with Aaron, she'd known where she stood. Like her *daed*, he'd praised her in one way or another. As the oldest of a growing family who strove to do everything right to gain her busy parents' attention, she'd craved affirmation. Although not proud of the need, Rachel recognized that praise had made her feel less invisible.

She blinked in the morning sun. Was that what prompted her to fall for Aaron? Certainly, he was very handsome, but really, when she thought about it, no more so than Benjamin. Had she been enamored by the way he automatically filled her subconscious need for validation with his flowery compliments?

Rachel considered the wall of green interspersed

with pale yellow blossoms in front of her. She wished she knew where she stood with Ben. Besides just as a responsibility. She wished she knew if her husband found her attractive. Because she did find him attractive. Rachel blushed at the acknowledgment. She might want words, but Ben's continual practice of doing things for her was starting to grow on her. Maybe her *mamm* was right. Words were sweet, but they didn't get things done. There were definitely many things that needed doing around a farmstead. To her surprise, she'd found doing those things brought a feeling of partnership to a couple. One more deeply rooted than one based on flowery words?

She certainly didn't feel invisible with Ben. She felt…cosseted. Was that because of responsibility to the mother of his children? Or because he cared for her as herself?

Rachel plucked a robust green cucumber at waist-height from a vine. Maybe she should tell Ben how much she appreciated his thoughtfulness. Things had been better between them lately. Weeks ago, he'd apologized about not trusting her. She'd understood. Given the situation, she'd have wondered the same thing.

She sighed. The rare kind word from Ben meant so much to her. Even though he never said anything, it probably worked in reverse. Her lips twitched. Was this part of the *work* in marriage her mother had referred to?

Adding the cucumber to her apron, she glanced over to where Ben was feeding the cattle. Rachel had to admit, he was certainly putting in the effort. He was always doing thoughtful things for her. If they were sitting at the table and she'd forgotten to put the butter on, before she could shift in her chair, he was up like a jack-in-the-box and rushing to the cupboard. When he was home, she couldn't climb into the buggy without his steadying hand under her arm, whether she needed it or not. When he wasn't home, and he found out she'd gone out, harnessing her horse by herself, he'd narrow his eyes in dismay. The next time she went to the barn, the harness was hung with lower pegs on the wall, making it easier to reach. He'd even mentioned getting a pony and cart for her to get around, reasoning that the babies would need one at some point anyway.

Snorting, Rachel worked her way down the fence to where she spied another cucumber hiding amongst the green leaves. How did he expect her to get around when he wasn't here if she didn't harness the horse and hook up the buggy? The babies hadn't affected her arms and legs. Although—she shifted at a twinge in her hips—they definitely were affecting other things. Still, it was sweet of him to be so attentive.

She should tell him. He wouldn't say anything, but his blue eyes might soften and his lips might lift in that endearing half smile she was beginning to watch for. A smile on her own lips, Rachel glanced again toward the cattle pen, where she could see Ben from the hip up as he walked along inside in the bunks, pouring something from the buckets he carried.

The cattle were jostling each other to get close to the feed. Her eyes narrowed as she noticed they were steering clear of the big bull, Billy. Through the rails of the fence, she could see slices of his large black profile. The bull's massive head was lowered. One cloven hoof was digging into the dirt, throwing clods of it over his shoulder.

Rachel's breath caught in her throat as she turned

to fully face the pen. A *rrumph, rrumph* bellow rumbled to her through the quiet summer morning. Openmouthed, Rachel's horrified gaze swiveled to where Ben had just climbed down from the last bunk and turned toward the barn, the empty pails swinging from his hands.

Frozen, Rachel watched the bull sprint across the pen. She willed herself to shout a warning, but no sound escaped her throat.

But something had alerted Ben. Turning at the last moment, he threw the pails toward the charging bull, giving him a second to try to dodge from its path. With a toss of Billy's colossal head, the pails went flying over his broad back. He struck Ben a second later.

Ben's hat sailed in one direction while he went flying in another. When he disappeared from her view, Rachel found her voice. She screamed so harshly, her throat was instantly raw. Rooted there in the garden, she kept screaming. Numb fingers dropped her apron. Vegetables scattered around her as she raised her hands to cup her face and scream, her horrified gaze locked on the pen. Through the space between the two lower boards of the fence, she saw a glimpse of Ben. He was belly-crawling toward the bunks along the side of the pen. Black-and-white legs milled around him as the steers tried to scatter from the wheeling bull.

Rachel's heartbeat pounded in her ears when she caught a flash of Ben's blue pants as he struggled to roll under the bunks amidst the churning feet. She shrieked anew when the bull slammed into the bunk. Unfazed, the huge Holstein rammed it again with his head. The sharp crack of splintering wood cut through the air.

A black blur flew into her peripheral vision. Gasping

through her burning throat at the fear it might be one of the other bulls, Rachel swiveled in its direction. Gravel flew as their neighbor's rig raced up the lane. Jethro Weaver launched himself from the buggy while it was still rolling. Yelling at the top of his lungs, he sprinted toward the fence. Whipping off his flat-brimmed hat, he threw it at Billy. With an ominous bellow, the animal turned in his direction. Jethro scrambled up the fence, continuing to yell at the big Holstein. Snagging a heavy stick leaning against a post, Jethro waved it at the bull. Shaking his massive head, Billy snorted. A few tense moments later, he lunged toward the shouting man. Keeping up his verbal onslaught, Jethro held his ground. With a final bawl, the bull veered off and trotted hostilely to the center of the pen.

Keeping his eye on the agitated animal, Jethro called over his shoulder. "Rachel! Rachel, can you hear m-me?"

"Ja." Rachel's mouth formed the word but she was voiceless. She'd screamed herself to hoarseness. Struggling to find enough saliva to swallow, she tried again, wincing at the pain in her throat as she got sound out. *"Ja."*

"Can you get in m-my rig? You need to ride d-down t-to the phone shack and call 911." Attention still on the pen in front of him, Jethro was slowly moving his way down the fence toward the bunks.

Only knowing the need for urgency kept Rachel from collapsing into the tilled earth of the garden. Bracing an arm under her stomach, she ran for the un-tethered buggy. The horse, in its confusion, had headed for the barn. Flinching at the rough gravel under her bare feet, Rachel raced across the driveway toward it.

She barely had breath for words as she clambered up the buggy steps. "Is he...?"

"Hurry, Rachel!"

Jethro's tone didn't invite further questions. Seizing the dangling reins, Rachel wheeled the buggy. She gasped as, from her perch, she spied Ben's motionless figure sprawled under a bunk. With a slap of the reins, the horse lurched down the lane. Careening onto the road, they raced the mile to the nearest phone shack.

Tumbling out of the buggy, Rachel barely caught herself when her feet hit the ground. She hadn't allowed herself to think during the frantic drive, just kept urging Jethro's Standardbred faster. She didn't stop to tie him. The horse's head was lowered as he panted for air, his bay coat flecked with lather.

Throwing open the shack's door with a bang, she stumbled inside. Her fingers trembled as she punched the emergency number. With an equally shaky voice, she relayed what she knew of the situation to the calm dispatcher.

Following the call, it took Rachel two attempts to get the handset back into its cradle. Once it rattled into place, she sagged against the bare wood wall of the shack. She'd told them what she knew, but what she didn't know was the status of her husband. Or if she still had one. They might rush out to find it was too late. She might be too late. *Oh, Ben, please let me have a chance to tell you how* wunderbar *a husband you've been, and what a* wunderbar *father I know you'll be.* Cradling her rounded belly, Rachel slid the rest of the way to the linoleum-covered floor.

Was he still alive? Please, please, *Gott*, let it be so. Tears flowed down her cheeks to drip onto her collarless dress. Her eyes squeezed tight at the memory of the shock, followed by wonder and joy in his face when he'd heard they were going to be parents of twins. Wonder and joy she'd shared. Quiet, endless support she'd known he'd give. Please, *Gott*…

The steady *clip-clop* of hooves gained in volume as someone passed by on the road. Sniffing, Rachel wiped her face on the sleeve of her dress and pushed to her feet. She wasn't doing any good here. Jethro might need her help. Ben—if he was alive—would need her. On shaky legs, she exited the phone shack. Jethro's horse, head up but still blowing slightly, eyed her warily.

"It's okay," she murmured, patting his sweaty side as she hurried past to the buggy. Please, *Gott*, let it be okay. Climbing onto the seat, she swung back onto the road. At a slightly less frantic speed, she drove back toward the farm.

The wail of a siren came up behind her. Rachel closed her eyes with a sigh of relief. Guiding the horse to the edge of the road, she pressed her lips together to keep from crying anew as a truck with a blue light flashing on its dash raced by. Recognizing Gabe Bartel's vehicle, she urged the horse to a faster speed. Turning into the lane, she slumped on the seat at the sight of Billy grazing placidly in the pasture with the steers. Somehow, Jethro had gotten him out of the pen. At least now they could safely reach Benjamin. But what would they find when they did?

Even burdened with the bags he carried, Gabe was scurrying up the rails of the fence when she drew the horse to a stop. Jethro waved him to where he stood by the bunk. Setting the buggy's brake, Rachel dropped the reins and scrambled down from the seat. Pressing a palm to the hitch in her side, she hurried over to where the bunks lined the fence. Kneeling, she peered between the first and second rails to see underneath the weatherworn wood of the feed bunks.

Ben lay motionless. His head was turned away from her.

"Is he…" She drew in a ragged breath, unable to finish.

At her voice, Ben groaned and slowly swiveled his face toward her. Rachel's heart ached as he obviously tried to give her a smile, any hint of dimple hidden in the smeared dirt on his cheek. She burst into tears at seeing him alive.

"Like…I…told…you…" There was no air behind his wheezing voice. He grimaced before continuing. "Don't…ever turn…your back…on a bull."

"That's good advice. Advice you should've taken." Gabe was working from Ben's other side. "Now for my advice. Let's not move until we have a better idea of what we're dealing with here." He ducked his head below the bunk to glance at Rachel. "The ambulance is on its way. Ben the bullfighter here needs some X-rays so we can determine the extent of internal injuries."

Rachel's eyes widened. Sniffing back her tears, she rubbed her wrist under her nose.

Watching her face through pain-hazed eyes, Ben flinched as he inhaled. "I don't…think…"

"Yeah, you're not thinking if you don't let us take you in. You need to be up and around to help her with those babies in a few months. For all I know, you hit your head. You're not in the best position to decide. So we'll consult the next of kin." Gabe glanced up from the gauge he was monitoring to meet Rachel's eyes. "Rachel?"

Her gaze traveled over Ben's white face and down the dirt-smeared shirt and pants of his sprawled and motionless body. One suspender strap dangled over his shoulder, its clasp broken. Swallowing, Rachel nodded. "I'll go down to the end of the lane and wave them in." Shifting from her knees to rock back on her feet, she used the rails of the fence to leverage up to a standing position.

She paused at the sound of Ben's feeble voice. "Don't…hurt…Billy. Bloodlines…too *gut*." Glancing over the bunk, she saw Jethro's lips thin as he shook his head.

Keeping a hand on the top rail, Rachel walked several yards down the fence until she felt steady enough to leave its support and cross to the driveway. Her eyes were focused on the sleek mostly black monster unconcernedly grazing in the pasture. For a moment, he became blurry as her face contorted and her eyes filled with tears. At the faint whine of a siren, she turned her head toward the road and hurried down to the end of the lane.

Chapter Eleven

Rachel rose from her chair when she saw the white lab-coated woman come through the gray swinging doors. Ben's *daed* leaped up, as well. Although they stayed seated, her *mamm* and Ben's dropped their knitting into their laps. Other members of the community who'd been trickling into the designated waiting room over the last hour halted their quiet conversations as they all turned toward the doors.

The gray-haired woman smiled at them. "You're here for Mr. Raber?" After their varying nods, she made eye contact with Rachel and motioned her closer. "Rachel Raber?" When Rachel hastened forward, the doctor continued in a lower voice, "Your husband is a very fortunate man. He has some broken ribs and a number of cracked ones. Although slightly bruised, his organs appear all right. Luckily, although there're some jagged edges, none of the fractures punctured a lung. He also has a badly sprained ankle, but considering he was outweighed more than ten to one, it could've been so much worse. Just to be on the safe side, we're going to keep him overnight to monitor his organs and lungs.

He'll be restricted in some movements for several days, and will be limited to lifting only a few pounds for several weeks, but should make a full recovery."

Clasping her hand to her mouth, Rachel closed her eyes and sagged against the wall. *Denki, Gott! Denki* that it was His will that Ben would live. Whether because of the coming *boppeli* or something else, she cared deeply for Ben. Was it love? It didn't matter. What mattered was that she now had a chance to find out.

She hadn't seen Ben since she'd watched with quaking limbs as the ambulance team braced his neck and carefully loaded him on a backboard for the trip to Portage. Gabe Bartel had given her a lift to her *mamm*'s house and had then taken them both to the hospital. When they'd arrived, Ben was nowhere to be found. Gabe, familiar with the facility and personnel, discovered Ben was being x-rayed. Rachel and Susannah had sat down to wait, joined shortly by Ben's parents, Elmer and Mary Raber.

"May I see him?"

"Absolutely," the older woman assured her, "he's been asking for you."

Rachel followed the doctor down the hall, her shoes squeaking on the shiny tile floor. When the doctor smiled and pushed open a wide door, pointing a thumb in its direction before heading on down the hall, Rachel peeked into the room. Her gaze immediately locked with Ben's. When he saw her, he shifted upright in the inclined hospital bed. He abruptly froze, his face going as white as the pillow supporting his dark-haired head. Rachel winced in sympathy before cautiously stepping into the room.

"Are you all right?" Focused on the unnatural beeps and hisses of the medical equipment, Rachel almost jumped at his quiet question.

She stopped along the raised silver rail that extended the length of the bed. "Am *I* all right? You're the one who was tossed like a doll by a bull."

He grimaced, then his face went slack as if he were concentrating before a dimple came into play along with a half smile. "Surely I looked more manly than that."

The tanned V of his neck, now displayed by the loose neck of his hospital gown, was in sharp contrast to the pale skin surrounding it. One of his always-capable arms was connected by tubes to a tall silver pole, a clear bag half-full of liquid suspended from its top. Another device was on a nearby pole, revealing lines and numbers in green. Without his always-present work shirt and suspenders, she barely recognized her husband.

"Well, your hat went one way and you went the other. Then I couldn't see you…" Rachel compressed her lips as her chin started to quiver. She squeezed her eyes tight against the prickling that threatened the backs of them. She didn't want to be a blubbery mess in front of him.

She opened her eyes at an abbreviated sigh from the direction of the bed. "I was afraid of that. That hat was just getting to be a perfect fit. I suppose there's no salvaging it?"

Sniffing, Rachel shook her head.

"Come here." Ben started to raise his arm before instantly stopping with an inhaled hiss. Rachel reached a hand through the rail of the bed and clasped his fingers where they'd returned to rest on the beige blanket.

Rotating his wrist to grasp her hand more fully, Ben returned the pressure. "I don't suppose this helps the way you feel about cattle."

Rachel snorted through her tears. "*Nee*. It doesn't help at all."

"Understandable." His lips twisted. "I suppose that means you won't be doing the cattle chores while I'm laid up for a few days?"

Tears were forgotten as her jaw dropped open. When she tried to jerk her hand back, he gently tightened his grip, keeping her fingers trapped.

"How could you think—" She paused at the sight of his smile.

"Stopped you from crying."

She sniffed again. "It isn't funny."

"I know." Releasing her fingers to carefully touch his side, he closed his eyes and sighed. "*Gut* thing, as I'm thinking it'll be a bit before I find the courage to try laughing."

Ben cautiously shifted his position on the bed. Rachel watched his face as flickers of reaction swept over it. He settled into place with a frown and lowered brow. He must be in terrible pain to reveal anything at all. Again, she sent up a silent prayer of thanks to *Gott* that, according to the doctor, Ben would make a full recovery. That time currently seemed far into the future.

"Your *daed* and *mamm* are here, along with several others. Your *daed* has already spoken with the bishop. He said not to worry about the bills. The church will figure out some way to pay for it."

Ben's frown deepened.

Rachel tried not to take pleasure in her next words. "And it'll probably be more than a few days before you're taking care of the cattle. The doctor said you'll be restricted for several days and won't be able to lift anything more than a few pounds for several weeks."

His eyes still closed, Ben grimaced more at this news than the physical pain when he'd moved abruptly. "She say when I'd be able to come home?"

"*Nee*. Not exactly. Only that they were keeping you overnight for observation."

Ben's eyes finally opened. "I doubt I'll be doing anything interesting enough that they'll find it worthwhile observing."

Rachel smiled at his feeble joke as he'd intended. "Do you want me to stay?"

After a quick glance around the sterile hospital room with its one stiff-looking chair, Ben frowned as he looked back at her. "*Nee*, I'd feel better if you went home. It'll be a more comfortable night for you there."

Focusing on keeping the hurt from her face, Rachel nodded slowly. He didn't want her there. He figured he'd be better without her. And why not, they didn't share a room at home. Their relationship was such that the overnight proximity would be both mentally and physically awkward. Dry-mouthed at the rejection, she forced a swallow. "I'll see you tomorrow morning then?"

"*Ja*. Hopefully with the doctor's permission to bring me home soon after. Will you be all right by yourself at the farm?"

"Of course." She shrugged half-heartedly. "I grew up on a farm. There were surely a few times I wouldn't have minded having the place to myself in order to have some peace and quiet. Besides, it's like a night off, as I don't have to fix you supper." Her joke must've been more feeble than his, as there was no ensuing lift of his lips.

"*Gut.* Hopefully you can get some rest. I'll see you tomorrow." There was a thread of gentleness in Ben's solemn voice as he held her gaze. Still, Rachel couldn't help but feel dismissed. With a jerky nod, she hurried out of the room. Entering the sterile corridor, her steps slowed when she saw the gathering of Amish community members in the waiting room. She hadn't asked Ben if he wanted more company. But she wasn't going back in there now. Resolutely, she headed for the expectant group. If he didn't want them, he'd have to turn them away himself. Just as he had her.

Ben's gaze was fastened on Rachel's straight back and the dangling ribbons of her *kapp* as they disappeared around the closing door. Shutting his eyes, he dropped his head back against the pillow. His face twisted in pain. Not the physical pain that stabbed through his body at any unwary move. That could be abated by the painkillers he suspected were dripping through tubes into his system. This ache was excruciating and would be harder to diminish. The hurt he'd seen in her face. The tears she'd shed. He'd caused them. Regardless if they were for him, or because of him, the fact he'd brought her distress pained him.

He shook his head against the pillow, about the only thing he could move right now without being jolted with breath-stealing reminders of why he was there. Despite his intent, he'd taken his wife's greatest fear and exacerbated it. Would she even want to stay on the farm? With his growing family, could he afford the higher rent if they had to move somewhere else or he no longer did chores for Isaiah?

Even if he could leave the hospital tomorrow—his aching chest clenched at the thought they wouldn't let him go—given the tightness of the skin he felt around his ankle and the twang of pain generating there whenever the sheets bumped his foot, he wouldn't be on his feet for a few more days.

The door swung inward. Opening his eyes, Ben eagerly lifted his head. Was Rachel returning? Had she determined to stay with him? At the sight of the white lab coat, he dropped his head back against the pillow.

The doctor quickly scanned the room. Her eyebrows rose. "Has your wife gone already? I thought she'd stay longer, as frantic as you were to see her."

Ben didn't have a reply.

"Well, can I trust you to follow instructions, or do we need her back here to ensure that you do?"

It depended what the instructions were. Ben forced a weak smile. "We're good."

The physician eyed him dubiously, gauging his sincerity before she began. "We don't wrap ribs anymore. We found it counterproductive. Although it might be uncomfortable, it's important to take occasional deep breaths and cough once in a while to prevent pneumonia. You'll have some whoppers of bruises. Most help we can offer on that is some pain medication and to recommend icing the area for a while." She frowned. "Do you have access to ice?" At his token nod, she continued, "You'll need to take it easy for several weeks. Be cautious on how much you lift in that time. Nothing very heavy."

"I don't want pain medication."

"I appreciate your concern, but we need to manage your pain enough that you can take deep breaths and cough occasionally. Not fully inflating your lungs is detrimental to their far ends. The blow you took probably bruised your lungs, which puts you at even higher risk of developing pneumonia, as the lung itself is injured. It might be painful at first, but I recommend you walk around the house several times a day if you can."

The information hit Ben harder than the bull had. "Around the house? I have work to do outside."

The doctor shook her head. "I wouldn't suggest it for the next four weeks at least. It usually will take six to eight weeks for a bone to heal."

"I can't." Ben shook his head at the absurd possibility.

"You can, unless you want worse problems." The physician pinned him with a pointed gaze over her glasses.

Ben closed his eyes as frustration swamped him. He'd always been the one who took care of things. Now he'd be a burden instead. How was he supposed to do cattle chores twice daily, along with anything else the animals might need? How was he supposed to do his work at Schrock Brothers' Furniture? How was he supposed to assist his wife and the ever-increasing burden she carried? Unthinking, he shifted in bed, hissing in a breath as he stiffened in shock at the pain that shot through him. His fingers curled around the smooth cool rails of the bed. Just the thought of trying to roll over made him sweat.

He opened his eyes to the doctor's sympathetic gaze. "We want to get you whole and back in business as soon as possible too, but you need to follow instruc-

tions to make it happen. I'll check back with you tomorrow morning and we can hopefully let you go then.
Do you have any questions?"

Ben shook his head wearily. None the doctor could
answer.

With a commiserating nod, the woman exited.
Beads of perspiration dotted Ben's forehead in the
air-conditioned room. Not only might he not be able
to take care of his own financial responsibilities, the
hospital stay made him a financial burden for others.
The Amish didn't carry health insurance. The community had always taken care of its members when they
were in need, somehow raising funds to cover costs.
They'd only just recently paid off hospital bills from
the bishop's heart attack episode earlier in the year. Ben
had always been on the giving end. He didn't know if
he could handle being on the receiving one.

How could his wife care for him if he failed in every
way of taking care of her?

With a scowl, Ben pushed against the cane to lever
out of his chair. He felt like a *grossdaddi*. Worse than
one. Because if he was old enough to be *en alder*, he
probably wouldn't be watching fretfully as his very expectant wife went out to hoe the garden, or wince when
she bent over to pick the green beans, or hold his breath
as she harnessed the horse. He should be doing work
for her, not causing her extra work. Shuffling to the
window, he looked out to where Jethro was feeding the
cattle. And that was another thing. Jethro had enough
to do at his own place. Having folks do things for him
when he should be doing them in reverse pained Ben
more than his sore ribs. He should be paying Jethro

the discount he was receiving for rent for the work he'd been doing these past few days since the incident.

Hands braced on the edge of the sink, Ben wedged himself higher so he could see over the rise of the hill in the pasture. There, grazing contentedly, was Billy. Even though the bull had hurt him, Ben was glad Isaiah Zook had been convinced not to sell the animal. Ben didn't want anyone else to be hurt, but he'd have felt worse if his carelessness in turning his back on the animal would've deprived Isaiah of good bloodlines to improve his dairy herd. But he understood Isaiah's dilemma. People had been killed before by rogue dairy bulls. It was frequently a one-and-done offense. The bull would be sold as he might be likely to do it again.

It was decided that Billy, until he was needed to sire cows, would be a fixture in the pasture and not in the pen with humans and the more docile steers. The two younger, smaller bulls kept him company.

Before climbing into his rig to drive down the lane, Jethro waved a farewell to Rachel, who stood leaning against her hoe in the garden. Ben turned from the window in frustration. His elbow banged against the plastic pail on the counter, shifting the five-gallon bucket closer to the edge. Jerking up a hand to catch it, Ben hissed in response to the pain that flared in his chest at the action, his fingers curling over the rim of the bucket.

When the pain ebbed, Ben stared at the bucket's contents. Extending one of the fingers curled over the pail's rim, he flicked the end of one of the green beans Rachel had picked earlier in the day that filled the bucket. His gaze shifted down the counter to the collection of clear quart jars, waiting to be sanitized and filled tomorrow when Rachel put up the beans.

Beans that weren't yet snapped.

Ben's eyes narrowed as he regarded the full bucket of green beans. His chest and foot might be bunged up, but his fingers still worked. Eyeing the pail, he gauged its weight. Too heavy for him to move. He snorted with disgust at his limitation in doing something he wouldn't have thought a moment about before. And the way his ankle was already starting to ache, he wouldn't even be able to stand up for long.

Glancing about the kitchen and living area for inspiration, his gaze landed on a tall stool. One that, to his apprehension, Rachel climbed to reach infrequently used items in the upper cupboards. If he could nudge it along the counter closer to the pail without twinging his ribs, it was tall enough that he could sit on it. It wasn't much, but at least snapping beans, he'd be of some use to someone.

Shuffling down the counter, Ben leaned to grab the stool's seat and immediately froze in place as his torso complained. Loudly. Resting his hands on the counter, he panted as he hooked a leg of the stool with the foot that had the bum ankle and tried to tug it toward him. He was glad Rachel wasn't in the house to hear the squeak he emitted at the flash of white-hot pain. Grimacing, he reevaluated the situation.

Working his way back down the counter, he snagged a large bowl from the dish drainer, along with a smaller one. Setting them on the counter in front of the stool, Ben limped back to the pail. Elbows protectively tight against his chest, teeth gritted in preparation of rogue pain spikes, he used both hands to carefully tip the bucket so green beans spilled over the counter toward the bowls. As he returned to the stool, Ben swiped more beans in that direction. With a sigh, he eased himself onto the stool and went to work, the *snap*, *snap*, *snap* of fresh green beans echoed about the otherwise empty kitchen while he watched his expectant wife work in the garden.

That was where Rachel found him when, hot, sweaty and with her back and hips aching more than she wanted to admit, she entered the kitchen. Her gaze shifted in amazement from the bowls and bowls of evenly snapped beans to the empty bucket sitting on the floor next to the door.

She slumped a hip against the doorjamb. "How?"

Ben rubbed his fingers together. "Billy didn't get ahold of these." He pointed farther down the countertop. "I saw you heading this way. There's a glass of lemonade for you by the refrigerator." Eyes on her face, he frowned. "You're flushed. You need to sit down."

Rachel nodded toward the sink, where the lunch dishes were now stacked haphazardly in the drainer. "What about you?"

"I've been sitting. And sitting. And sitting." Quickly masking a grimace, Ben levered off the chair. "So why don't you sit for a minute with your drink. I don't promise that it'll be much more than just edible, but I'll find us something to eat for supper." He grinned, his dimples making a brief appearance. "It just won't be green beans. I'm tired of looking at them."

Rachel picked up the glass before gratefully sinking into the chair at the table. Taking a deep drink of lemonade, she raised her eyebrows at the tartness of it—Ben had a heavy hand with the powdered mix—but the taste was perfect for how hot and tired she was. Sighing in contentment, she scanned the cluttered countertop. It looked like he'd used every bowl in the kitchen to contain the snapped beans. Rachel didn't care. She'd been dreading spending the evening snapping beans. A task that needed to be done, but not one she cared for. She'd much rather pod peas. Actually tonight, she'd much rather sit and do nothing. Or just hand sew the little outfits she'd been making for the babies. And now she could.

Taking another sip, she studied Ben's back, broad between the bands of his suspenders and his lean, corded forearms, the dark tan of them sharply contrasting with the rolled up sleeves of his white shirt as he pulled a carton of eggs from the refrigerator. His brother, Aaron, might have frequently filled her ears and soul with sweet words, but right now, Rachel couldn't think of anything sweeter or more satisfying for her body and soul than what her husband had just done for her.

Chapter Twelve

"It pains me to watch you walk across the room, so I can't imagine how you're feeling." Ben's eyes were worried when Rachel glanced over at his comment.

She shifted her unconscious grimace into a weak smile. "Well," she pressed one hand against what seemed the constant ache in her back and hips and the other under her greatly rounded midsection, "I must admit, it pains me too."

"Why don't you sit down?" Ben patted the chair he was passing. "How long before…they arrive?"

"They'll come when they're ready. But the midwife says that twins usually arrive three weeks or so before single babies. It's September so maybe in another few weeks?" Her tentative glance met his.

Ben's eyes widened. He looked down at her stomach, then back to meet her gaze. Rachel knew what he was thinking. She was thinking the same thing. How much bigger would she get before the babies came? How much bigger *could* she?

"Do you—" he swallowed "—do you regret not

doing the pictures and procedures like the *Englisch* people do?"

Stifling a groan as she shifted position, Rachel twisted her hands together. "It's not our way. I don't care whether they're boys or girls, but—" she started to inhale deeply, flinching when she was reminded it wasn't possible to do so anymore. "I'd like to know how they're doing. To know they're…all right." Her voice ended as breathless as she felt.

"I know. But whatever happens, it's *Gott*'s will." Ben quietly echoed her thoughts.

Rachel steered her mind away from what wasn't hers to control. "And I can't sit. There's too much to do."

"I can help."

"*Nee.* When? You returned to work weeks ago, probably sooner than you should've. Now that the doctor reluctantly cleared you to feed the cattle after six weeks, with that and all the other livestock chores you persuaded Jethro to leave for you." She shook her head. "You won't have time for much more."

"You need some help. We'll need to hire a helper after the babies are born anyway. How about hiring one now?"

Rachel blinked at the possibility. Employing a hired girl after a baby's arrival was common practice in the Amish community. Rachel didn't know about having one come before the child was born, but the way her hips and back constantly bothered her and the sleep she wasn't getting at night was beginning to wear on her. She shuffled over to the chair Ben had indicated earlier and sank down into it.

"Who would you suggest?"

Ben sat down in his chair as he pondered the question. "Your *schweschder*?"

Rachel shook her head. "Rebecca likes her job at the restaurant. She's worked there for years. I couldn't ask her to quit to help me for a short time and risk not getting her job back."

"*Ach*, the same with mine. With two of us in the family recently gone—" Rachel shared his wince at the words, knowing he was referring to Aaron "—they're needed at home, at least until winter."

They sat in silence. Rachel figured Ben, like her, was trying to think of available young women in the community.

Ben straightened in his chair. "Jacob mentioned at work that his sister was looking for a job. Perhaps…"

"I don't think so."

Ben grinned at her quick denial and flat tone. "No?" Rachel could see his dimples flash. She raised her eyebrows at him so he knew she didn't appreciate his teasing.

"No," she reiterated empathically.

"Why ever not, I wonder." Folding his hands together, Ben thoughtfully considered the ceiling.

Rachel snorted. "I'd rather do everything myself before and after the *boppeli* are born than have Lydia Troyer in my house." Just the thought made her want to shudder. "Besides, do you want everyone in the district to know what goes on in our house?"

Ben was still smiling when he glanced back at her. "I'm sure someone will come to mind before we have to resort to certain considerations. But as far as gossip, it's not like we're really that interesting…" His voice trailed off as his gaze touched on their separate bedroom doors. "I suppose not."

Rachel's attention rested on the wooden doors as well. What would happen after the *boppeli* were born? Would she and Ben continue to stay in separate rooms? Shifting in her seat, she carefully avoided looking at him as she felt her cheeks warm. Now, the way she constantly twisted and turned in a futile attempt to find a comfortable position for the night, she'd keep anyone else in the room awake, as well. But after the *boppeli* arrived... Rachel flushed further as she realized she wouldn't mind sharing a bedroom with her husband. The two rooms, an embarrassing and adamant necessity when they'd moved in immediately after their awkward wedding, now didn't seem quite as necessary. Needing to do something with her hands, Rachel picked up the dark blue cloth on the petite table next to her chair and searched it until she located her sewing needle.

"Probably a *gut* thing about Lydia."

Frowning at the mention of the woman's name and the memories it stirred, Rachel looked over in question at Ben's overly casual remark.

"As Jacob said the job she's looking for is in Pennsylvania."

Rachel sat forward abruptly, or tried to with the burden of her stomach. "What?"

"Going there to live with a cousin. Seems she thinks the opportunities might be more plentiful there."

Rachel's lips twisted, although they were on their way to a smile. "The opportunities to chase men, you mean."

"Think I ought to warn them?" Ben picked up the

paper from the small table beside his chair. "I could run an advertisement in *The Budget*. Sort of like a public service announcement."

Her chuckle expanded to a laugh, followed by a groan when she couldn't find enough air to support her giggles. "*Nee*. She might be just what someone is looking for."

"That's a frightening thought. Even to inflict on Pennsylvanians."

Rachel giggled some more, her hands bouncing on her rounded belly. When she regained composure, she mused, "I hope for even Lydia to find her chosen one. She wants a husband very much."

Ben met her smiling gaze. "Well, we don't always get what we want." If the room weren't so quiet, she wouldn't have heard his following words as he lifted the paper and turned his attention to it. "Although sometimes it's possible."

Rachel continued to study him, her smile softening. Although she certainly hadn't thought it at the time, she was realizing more and more that Ben was surely *Gott*'s chosen one for her. She was sure she'd been in love with Aaron. But Ben just grew on you over time. Her hands on her stomach shifted to identify a knee here, an elbow over there. Kind of like her little passengers. Who would soon be arriving.

Refocusing on potential hired girls, Rachel considered the young women in the community. But any that came to mind either had jobs, were needed at home or were perhaps too young. Which was quite young indeed, as many Amish girls in large families were already well accustomed to taking care of younger siblings and household chores at an early age.

Ben's sigh drifted to her as she picked up her sewing.
He was apparently running into the same roadblock.
With his work-roughened hand, he began stroking his
short beard. Rachel hid a smile at the sight. After all
these months, he still didn't seem used to its presence.
But, seeing his eyes narrow as he stared at the wall,
perhaps the action was thought-provoking.

"Gideon Schrock mentioned wanting to get one of
his sisters up to Wisconsin. He's been living at the farm
with Samuel and Gail since they were married, but
Gideon figures when they start growing their family,
they'll want the place to themselves. He's not opposed
to moving out, but not if he has to fix his own meals
and take care of housework." Ben grinned. "Apparently, he and Samuel weren't too successful at that before. But if a sister moved up, they could share a place."

Rachel paused in the middle of a stitch. She liked
the Schrock brothers, who'd moved into the area a few
years back when Malachi Schrock had purchased the
furniture business where Ben worked. If the sister was
anything like her brothers, Rachel figured they could
deal pretty well together.

"Weren't they from Ohio? Do you think she'd move
that far from home to come up here?"

"I don't know. I'll ask Gideon or Malachi. From
what he said, I know Gideon would be all for it. Do you
think she'll be able to care for two *boppeli*?"

Wrinkling her nose, Rachel resumed her sewing. "I
don't know how well I'll be able to care for two *boppeli* and I'm going to be their *mamm*."

"I think you'll be a *wunderbar mamm* to them."

Rachel flushed under his warm regard. Her husband
may not say sweet words to her very frequently, but

when he did, she knew they were heartfelt and all the more precious. Her gaze darted about the picked-up living area, cleaning that she hadn't done. Another thing he just quietly did for her. Ben's kind words might be the frosting on the cake of all she was discovering he did for her. And, to Rachel's surprise, she was discovering, between the two, she'd rather have the cake.

Rachel's heavy sigh echoed across the quiet room. Ben looked up from reviewing local livestock sales listed in *The Budget*. Someday, when they had their own place, he'd liked to get a few cattle. If his wife could tolerate them. "What's wrong?"

"I left my scissors in the bedroom." Shifting awkwardly, she placed her hands on the edge of the chair to lever herself up.

Ben was relieved the twinge that stung his chest when he bounded out of his seat was minimal. "You stay put. I'll get it."

"Denki," she murmured gratefully as she sank back into her chair with a soft smile.

"Where am I looking?" Ben called over his shoulder as he headed for her bedroom.

"I was working the other night when I couldn't sleep. Should be somewhere on the stand by the bed? Maybe in the drawer?"

When he lit the lamp on the nightstand, the only other items on the otherwise neat surface were a spool of thread and a half-finished outfit, similar to the one she was currently working on in the other room. Ben smiled. Rachel had started two, reasoning that, with twins, many outfits would need to be completed. Having projects in both rooms saved walking back and forth if she happened to carefully settle where one wasn't within reach. Lifting the dark blue fabric to confirm the scissors weren't hidden underneath, Ben marveled at its miniature size, at the wonder that it could soon hold his son or daughter. He was flooded with emotions he wasn't yet ready to share with his wife. Tempted, as things had been so *gut* between them lately, but not yet ready.

Closing his eyes, he brought the tiny garment to his chest and pressed it against his heart. Gott, denki *for this dream I never figured could be realized. The chance to love this woman. To raise a family with her. Although I feared at first, I believe that we can make it. That in time our marriage can thrive and not just exist.* His fingers tightened around the garment. *That these will be the first of many children. Help me to be the husband and* daed *I need to be.*

Raising the fabric to his face, he pressed his lips to it before carefully setting it down. Not finding the scissors on top of the nightstand, he tugged on the nob of the simple single drawer below. It slid out easily, revealing the scissors and a few spools of thread. Relieved at the discovery, Ben picked them up and started to slide the drawer shut. He froze when he saw what lay beneath the scissors.

Inside the drawer, its few contents neat like the surface of the stand, was an envelope. Instantly recognizing the handwriting that scrawled Rachel Mast across the front of it, Ben's breath had locked in his throat. As brothers sharing a desk at school, they used to tease each other. Aaron had liked to write as much as Ben hadn't. Sometimes he would write Ben's homework for him in exchange for Ben doing chores. Until the teacher noted Aaron's handwriting, as Ben did now.

After a moment, his eyes shifted to the empty white corner. No return address.

His *bruder* had written his wife. And she hadn't said anything about it.

Unconsciously straightening, Ben put a few more inches between him and the drawer, his eyes still fixed on its contents. When had the letter been sent? The postmark was smudged. Had she brought it over when they'd moved? It was addressed to her family's farm. It could be an old communication. Aaron was good about that. Writing letters. Saying sweet things. They'd had a long romance. Aaron could've sent several letters and she'd only kept this one. That was history.

But still, she'd kept this one.

His heart rate accelerated as his stomach twisted. Things seemed to have been going so well between them lately.

He shouldn't look at it.

But it could be recent. It could reveal where his *bruder* was. What he was doing. Ben reached toward it, his hand pausing an inch away. If it was recent, it could be something he didn't want to see. What could be good about his wife communicating with the man she'd thought she'd marry? What could be good about her keeping secrets from her husband?

Ben jerked his hand back. He swallowed before snorting softly. He'd been less cautious when he'd once encountered a rare Massasauga rattlesnake while clearing brush.

"Did you find it?" He flinched as Rachel's voice floated in from the other room.

"Ja." He responded hoarsely. He'd found it, all right.

He'd rather deal with the snake. Tentatively, as if it was the poisonous reptile, he lifted the envelope and turned it over. It was open. Whatever was in it, Rachel had read it. She knew what it said. His breathing shallow, Ben opened the flap and pulled out the single sheet of paper. Flicking it open, one ear tuned to the door in case Rachel decided to see what was keeping him, he scanned the words. His *bruder* had written so little. Said so much. Folding the paper with a slow exhale, Ben returned it to the envelope.

No word of where his brother was. Only that he was thinking about Ben's wife and regretted hurting her. No word of whether he was coming back. It'd been sent to Rachel's home address. Did he know she was married? Did Aaron know Ben had taken his wife? His life?

Speaking of secrets, didn't Ben have his own? His hand clenched, reminding him of the forgotten scissors when the edges of the blade cut into his palm. Slowly, carefully, he pushed the drawer shut. Rachel was to have been Aaron's wife. Her children should've been Aaron's. He'd stolen his brother's life.

Gott's opinion on coveting was well-known. Ben swallowed as he backed away from the stand. His silent prayer now was quite different. May *Gott* forgive him for what he'd done. Hopefully sooner than he could forgive his wife and himself. As for his brother? If he returned, Ben didn't figure Aaron would ever forgive him.

"Denki. You're a tremendous help to me. I'm fortunate to have you." Rachel's words drifted over her shoulder as she worked at the sink.

Ben paused in the action of clearing the supper table to absorb her words. They warmed him like a glowing stove in January, particularly after finding the letter two weeks ago. His lips twisted. When had he become so maudlin? You'd think he was now the one with child, he was so out of balance with emotions.

He watched Rachel shift her position a few times before she plucked another tomato from the sink. Remembering Hannah's words that it would help his pregnant wife to be off her feet, he frowned as he crossed to the counter.

"Are you doing too much so late in your condition?" He nodded toward the collection of already full jars farther down the counter and the sink full of tomatoes.

Rachel's expression was bland. But Ben knew she'd become quite adept at masking her discomfort over the past several weeks. "It's not work when you like doing it."

"You like doing this?" His tone revealed his surprise.

"Oh, *ja*. It gives me great pleasure to see the shelves filling up with food for the winter. In fact, if Isaiah doesn't mind, I'd like to expand the garden next year."

Ben grunted as he retrieved another paring knife from the drawer and joined her at the sink. She shifted to make room. He reached in the water for a tomato and began to peel. "We might have to buy our own draft horses if I expand it much more."

Rachel grinned. "If we expand, I can add some different vegetables and herbs or plant more of what I did this year so I'd have enough to sell." She looked up at him with such enthusiasm in her face that Ben would've put the horse collar on his own shoulders and tugged the plow across the ground himself just to keep her expression in place.

"Then I can help earn some money. Maybe to get a place of our own sooner?"

"You just want a place where you can put in an even bigger garden. Sounds like it needs at least forty acres of cleared flat ground just for your vegetables. I guess I need to make that a four-horse team and get a cultivator as well as disk and plow."

She giggled.

He shared her smile as he dropped the peeled tomato into the bowl with the others. It warmed him to be talking about the future with her. Talking and smiling about plans she had. Plans that included him. Reaching into the sink for another tomato, Ben froze when his hand connected with Rachel's grabbing the same bobbing target. She went still, as well. Striving to control his suddenly elevated breathing, he carefully loosened his fingers to seek out another objective. Plucking one, he shook the water from it and began to peel. Plans that included him only because his brother was no longer in the picture.

Ben's hand tightened on the tomato as he recalled the letter. With a squirt of juice, it slipped from his fingers and fell back into the water with a plop. "Sorry," he muttered. Fishing it out again, he scrapped the knife across its surface, peeling off the skin that'd been loosened by the blanching. Who knew when that letter had been sent? Although he'd always been aware of their actions while they were courting, he hadn't been involved in her and Aaron's relationship. They could've had a falling out before and the letter had been sent when Aaron was still living at home.

Since he'd found the letter, he'd given Rachel ample opportunity to mention it. All without mentioning Aaron. He'd dropped associated topics. Discussed letters that'd come in the mail. She'd never said a word. It only made him worry more. Ben thought about his last interaction with Lydia. He would never break his vows. But if Aaron ever came back, would Rachel? Would she meet secretly and intimately with his *bruder*? Would she betray him that way? Would Aaron? Grimly, Ben remembered that he, not Aaron, was the cowbird that came in to steal the nest Rachel had been planning to build with a husband.

But Rachel was now smiling while talking about future plans with him. Surely that meant something?

He slid a sideways glance at her. Tendrils of her hair, damp from the steamy heat of canning, curled about her flushed face. One clung to her cheek. Her hands busy, Ben watched as she tried to blow it free with a puff from pursed lips. Lips he wanted to kiss. But the situation never seemed right and, his stomach churned as the letter and what it might mean had taken root in his mind, she might not want his affection. Ben didn't know what made him feel worse, that she would avoid any overtures he might make, or that she would accept them unwillingly. Either way, he would keep his hands and lips to himself, if not his heart. It was too late for that.

Searching for distraction from his dismal thoughts, he glanced out the window. In the pasture, Billy was wrestling with one of the smaller bulls. Head to head, the big bull easily pushed the lighter one back. With a final lunge, he knocked the other to its knees. Ben stiffened, watching carefully as the smaller bull scrambled to its feet and scampered safely away from the big animal.

Rachel glanced out the window in the direction of his gaze. Ben heard her disturbed sigh when she noticed the bull.

"I wished you hadn't started doing chores again."

"The doctor said my ribs were healed enough to handle lifting the weight of the pails. Besides, I didn't want to put Jethro out any more than I had already."

Any sign of smiles was gone. Her lips were tight as she dropped her tomato into the bowl and jerked another one from the water. "I liked it better when Isaiah took Billy to his place for a while. I was sorry to see him come back."

Putting his tomato in the bowl, Ben picked up another. "The cows needed him. I'm glad Isaiah didn't sell him. I made a mistake. Billy made a mistake. We're even. I'd feel bad if I'd deprived Isaiah of good genetics when I'm supposed to be the one taking care of the animals."

"The cows might need him, but I need to see him as hamburger. He could've killed you."

Ben's lips twitched, secretly delighted with her concern. "He'd be a lot of hamburger. Almost enough to go with all your canned tomatoes."

To his regret, she didn't smile at his joke. "Speaking of which, I'll need more jars from the basement. I'll go get them if you want to finish these up?"

Putting his finished tomato in the bowl, Ben set down his knife and rinsed his hands by swishing them through the water. "I'll get them. I don't want to think about you going down those steep stairs any more than you have to. Or coming back up with a boxful of jars. Quarts or pints?"

"Quarts. We're a growing family." This time a smile accompanied her words.

He raised his eyebrows. "Not growing that fast. I hope these keep a few years. I'm thinking the *boppeli* won't be eating tomatoes for a while."

"Okay," she relented. "A mixture of quarts and pints."

He dried his hands on a nearby dish towel. "Why didn't you plan a canning frolic here with some of your friends? I know you've been to a few this summer."

She wrinkled her nose. "Maybe next year. This year, I just wanted to settle into my own kitchen. I know some folks have bigger dreams, but mine was always just to have my own home, sharing it with children and—" She halted abruptly as she stared down at the tomato in her hand. "And taking care of it and them," she finished awkwardly.

Ben strode to the basement door and jerked it open. "I'll get the jars," he tossed over his shoulder. He descended the stairs to the concrete-floored basement, his heart as heavy as his tread, his mind echoing with the word she didn't say. That she was going to say. *My own home, sharing it with children and... Aaron.*

Rachel watched as Ben disappeared through the door to the basement. She'd been so glad she'd caught herself in time. Before she finished with, *and the man I love.* Because she was beginning to think she loved Ben. But she wasn't ready to share that, as he hadn't given any indication he felt the same way.

He'd been quiet lately. Ben was generally quiet, but

he'd seemed particularly withdrawn lately. Was he worried about being a *daed*? Dropping the last tomato into the heaping bowl, she bent and leaned an elbow on the edge of the sink. Now that he wasn't watching, she reached to press a hand against the small of her back, which had been aching for some time. Along with her hips, but that was nothing new. They'd been aching for the past month, particularly the past two weeks.

Not only Ben, but the *boppeli* were quieter, as well. What was it with her family recently? They'd been as active lately as Standardbreds coming down the home stretch, but today, their movements were more subdued. Rachel smiled faintly. She could tell them apart. She didn't know who they were yet, or, she grimaced ruefully, what they would be called—another thing she and Ben hadn't talked about—but she could tell who was where. Not only had they not talked of names, but Ben had never felt them move. Other than that first time just after they'd learned there were two when he'd seemed intrigued, he hadn't indicated an interest. Sure, she'd catch his gaze on her in the evenings when she'd exclaim after one of the *boppelis'* particularly rambunctious bouts, but he'd never said a word and, although she'd wanted to share their movements, she was afraid to ask if he was interested. In case he wasn't. In case, although he seemed to be tolerating their marriage, he wasn't really excited about the reason it had come about. At least, not like Rachel was. She couldn't wait to see their little faces. To hold them in her arms. To assure herself they weren't affected by what had taken her two siblings. As another spasm surged across her back, she pressed her hand more forcefully against her spine and bit her lip.

Hearing Ben's step ascending the stairs, Rachel straightened from her slouch against the sink and smoothed her features. Pulling the sink's plug, she drained the initially cool water where the tomatoes had been transferred after their hot water blanching.

"Find some?" Efficiently cleaning out the sink, she prepared to wash the new jars.

Jars rattled in the cardboard box as Ben carried them over. "You and your *mamm* must've hit every auction this spring and summer to collect so many of these. Did you outbid everyone in the district?"

Glancing over as he set the box down on the counter, Rachel assessed whether he was truly upset. Seeing a welcomed hint of his dimple, she began putting the jars in the rising soapy water. "Only the ones that weren't quick enough. I hope you don't mind. I told *Mamm* I'd share some of the canning so she wouldn't have to put up as much. I used to do it at home as she was busy with the goats and bees. She has a new hired hand now." Rachel frowned as she washed and rinsed a jar and set it upside down in the drainer to dry. "But I don't know that he's working out that well."

She raised her eyebrows when Ben picked up a dish towel and began to dry the jar. "Well, I hope Miriam Schrock works out for us. Gideon said the other day that he was picking her up from the bus station tonight." Setting the dried jar on the table, Ben reached for another one from the drainer. "I think, or at least hope that she was a good choice as a hired girl. If she's anything like Malachi, Samuel and Gideon, I'm sure she'll work out fine. Still, I look forward to getting to know her a bit before the *boppeli* arrive and she moves in."

Under the concealing suds, Rachel clenched her hand around a pint jar as another spasm seared her back. She panted quietly through pursed lips. She was afraid they might not have a chance to even meet Miriam before the *boppeli* arrived.

Chapter Thirteen

"Ben…"

Instantly awake, Ben sat up at the sound of Rachel's voice outside his bedroom door.

"Coming," he called as he swung his feet to the floor. Flicking on the flashlight on his nightstand, he pointed it at the small clock there. It wasn't so much the time that concerned him—shortly after midnight—it was the tone of her voice. The tight, anxious tone. Hastily he donned his clothes and was swinging open the door a moment later.

Her tone—and her face. Rachel's face, its paleness emphasized by the fall of her dark hair that framed it, was tight with pain in the glow of the lamp she held. Garbed in the loose gown above her bare feet, she bit her lip as her wide eyes met Ben's.

When she grasped his hands, he was surprised at the crushing pressure of her fingers. "The midwife?"

She nodded.

Lifting their clasped hands to his lips, Ben kissed the slender back of his wife's. "I'll be back from the phone booth as fast as I can."

When he would've let go, Rachel clung to his hand. "I want my *mamm*."

Ben hissed in a thoughtful breath. While it was only a mile down to the local phone shack, it was several more miles to Susannah Mast's farm. He didn't want to leave Rachel alone long enough to travel there and back. Opening his mouth to say so, he slowly closed it again at the pleading evident in her dark eyes.

"*Ach*, I already owe Jethro more than I could ever pay. I might as well add this to the list. I'll see if he'll go to your farm and bring your *mamm* here to you. Is that agreeable?"

Grimacing, she hunched over in mid-nod. Wincing himself, Ben helped her back into her bedroom and assisted her onto the bed. "I shouldn't be gone too long. Do you need anything before I go?"

"Just Mrs. Edigers and my *mamm*." As he loosened his arms from about her, Rachel reached up to palm his cheek. "And you."

He was momentarily stunned at the words and the touch of her hand. Once she removed it, Ben nodded so hard he was afraid his head would snap off his neck. Leaving her on the bed, he rushed to the door, only to stop and turn when he reached it. "I'll be right back."

Dashing out the front door, he was halfway down the sidewalk before he quickly retreated to put on his shoes. A short minute later, he was bridling Sojourner before launching himself on the back of the startled mare. At his urging, the confused horse broke into a gallop as soon as they cleared the barn.

"I'll probably never get you back to just trotting with the buggy," Ben muttered into the mane flying into his face as he leaned over her neck. "I can live with that, if you get us there and back double quick tonight." After the breathless moonlight run, he vaulted from Sojourner's back as she slid to a stop in front of the phone shack.

Flinging the shack's door open, he was dialing the phone a second later. Mrs. Edigers's number was taped inside the phone shack, useless in the current darkness of the booth. Fortunately, Ben had the digits memorized from the first time they'd met with the woman. The midwife answered on the second ring.

"The *boppeli* are coming!" Ben didn't identify himself, but either Mrs. Edigers recognized his voice or she'd noted the plural.

"I'll grab some things and contact Hannah."

Ben recalled how restless Rachel had been when he'd come home from work yesterday. Several times over the evening before they'd gone to their separate bedrooms, he caught her absently rubbing her back. He'd seen her struggle through various discomforts in the past months. Her face tonight told him she'd been in pain for quite a while. "I think she's been… I think this has been going on a while."

"Hmm. All right, we'll be there shortly."

At her calm, steady voice, Ben took his first normal breaths since hearing Rachel's tense summons at his bedroom door. Hanging up the phone, he stepped out of the booth. Fortunately, Sojy hadn't wandered off following her wild ride when he'd dropped the reins. Patting her neck, he gathered up the leads and swung onto her back. He turned her in the direction of Jethro Weaver's small farm, another mile farther up the road.

Although it took a moment for his neighbor to come to the door, Jethro immediately swung it wide upon seeing Ben. He began putting on his shoes as Ben explained why he'd burst in on him in the middle of the night. Without further question, Jethro headed to the barn. Mission accomplished, Ben leaped back onto Sojy and sped home.

Trusting the mare wouldn't go any farther than the barn if she wandered, Ben left her at the yard gate and raced into the house. Panting, more from suppressed tension than expended energy, he halted at her partially closed door.

"Rachel?" His intended whisper came out much harsher than intended in his concern.

"Come in." He swung the door open to see her neatly stacking the nightstand with towels, sheets and other paraphernalia. His eyes widened to discover she'd changed into the white birthing gown she'd shyly made in the last few weeks. Her hair was now neatly pinned under a *kapp*.

"Are you all right?"

"*Ja*. Just glad you're back. Is my *mamm* coming?"

"Jethro's on his way there now. The midwife's on her way too." He scrutinized her from the doorway. Although flushed and sweaty with slight anxiety in her eyes, she otherwise appeared calm. "If you'll be okay for the moment, I need to take care of Sojy." At her nod, he turned from the door, only to spin back around at the breathless sound of his name.

"Ben, we're finally going to meet them. I can't believe we'll be parents soon."

Sharing her bemused smile before he ducked out of the doorway, Ben found himself nodding giddily as well as he crossed to the door.

Although he'd only been back in the house a few

minutes after tending to the mare, it seemed like forever before Ben heard a car in the drive, alerting him that help had arrived.

He met them at the door. Mrs. Edigers and Hannah Bartel gave him encouraging smiles as they hurried past, laden with equipment. When they disappeared through Rachel's door, he paced the living room, listening for the clatter of hooves on the driveway that would hopefully mean Jethro had been successful in delivering Rachel's mother.

When they arrived thirty minutes later, Ben was out in the yard in time to help Susannah down from the buggy. Her searching look at Ben was seemingly satisfied with his ragged nod. The sight of the midwife's car made her more so.

"Don't go too far," she instructed him as she crossed the porch. "You'll be needed as a catcher. Even more important when there are two."

Both men's gazes followed her into the house. At the click of the door behind her, Ben turned to Jethro. "*Denki*. I can't thank you enough for bringing her."

"Glad t-to help."

"Seems I can't thank you enough, period, Jethro. I don't know what I'd do without you lately."

"It's what neighbors are for." The man brushed off the gratitude. "You'd d-do the same for m-me."

"Whenever I have the chance. Do you want to come in?"

Glancing at the door, Jethro shook his head like inside the house was the last place he wanted to be. "*Nee*. I need t-to get home."

Although he wanted to be with Rachel whenever

she might need him, Ben understood the sentiment. "Can I get you anything before you go?"

"*Nee*. I'm *gut*." Before turning his horse down the lane, Jethro cast another look at the house.

Ben furrowed his brow at the obvious longing in the man's gaze, until he remembered Jethro had lost a wife and unborn child. The realization was a blow to his midsection. Pivoting from the rig already clattering away, he hurried into the house and quietly crossed to Rachel's bedroom door to peek inside.

There was an intense purposefulness in the room. To his relief, the three women appeared calm and confident in their actions. A glance at Rachel's contorted red face however, escalated his concern.

Seeing him hover in the doorway, Mrs. Edigers motioned Ben inside. "Go wash up well with plenty of soap." She swept a gaze over his attire, which Ben knew was soiled from his quick journey and care of Sojourner. "And put on a clean shirt."

Ben hastened to do as instructed, his heart beating so rapidly his fingers fumbling over the fastenings in the transition. Up to this point, the *boppeli* seemed real in an abstract manner as they'd prepared. Rachel had sewn blankets and several sets of clothes for them. He'd made two cradles, mainly while he was laid up from doing other things. Although he'd seen his wife touch her middle with an expression of wonder on her face when she'd felt them move, he hadn't had the courage to ask to feel them himself, and she hadn't offered. The babies' existence had just primarily been the unlikely reason he and Rachel had married.

Now with their imminent arrival, the realization

there'd soon be two little ones in the house, depending on him, shook him to the core.

Failing twice to get the clean shirt fastened, Ben held his hands before him, dismayed at their trembling. He, who was steady and sure with detail work in furniture making, in fact was steady and sure in most aspects of his life except being a husband, couldn't fasten a shirt. Whereas Rachel had grown up caring for little ones, how could he handle being a *daed* to not just one but two? Drawing in a shaky breath when he heard Mrs. Edigers call his name, he tackled the task a third time. He was about to find out, whether he was ready or not.

A short time later, Ben held his tiny son. Although he squirmed, the little one didn't make a sound. Mrs. Edigers quickly took the baby from Ben's dazed hands. The midwife's back was turned to Ben when he heard what sounded like the bleat of a baby goat. He looked over Mrs. Edigers's shoulder to see her and Hannah vigorously rubbing the baby with a towel. Ben's heart clinched as he caught the look the midwife shared with Hannah as they bent over the little one, attending to its immediate needs.

There was trouble. He was too small. They didn't think his son was going to make it.

"I want to see my *boppeli*." Rachel struggled to sit up.

Wrapping the baby in a clean blanket, Mrs. Edigers carried him to the head of the bed. "For a brief moment. We aren't done yet. You've got some more work to do."

If he hadn't loved her already, Ben would've fallen hard as he watched Rachel take their child into her arms and look down at his tiny face with a sense of wonder. Ben dodged the others until he was beside her at the head of the bed. Determining the bustling women in the room were busy with other tasks, Ben leaned down and gently kissed Rachel's hair, visible before the edge of her *kapp*.

He had to tell her. "I love you" he mouthed, knowing he was safe, that Rachel wouldn't see his words as she was focused on their tiny son in her arms.

She looked up, almost catching him. "Do you want to hold him?"

Ben's heart thundered in his chest. After confirming the midwife's approval, he nodded. He couldn't even speak to the affirmative. Silently, Rachel handed their son to him. He felt like reverse gravity, the miniature bundle was so light. It seemed impossible that a son, *his* son, who would someday stand shoulder to shoulder with him, was wrapped up inside.

If *Gott* willed it.

He forced himself not to tighten his arms in protection around his precious bundle, afraid he might accidentally crush his oldest child. This tiny person, who surely weighed no more than the dandelion fluff that blew through the pasture. *Please don't blow through my life that fast. I know whatever happens is* Gott*'s will, but I hope His will is that you grow strong and tall to work beside me.* The *boppeli*'s hands were tucked under his chin, just visible at the top of the blanket. In awe, Ben brushed the newborn skin with the tip of his finger. Tiny fingers with delicate fingernails moved to curl partway around his calloused thumb.

Mrs. Edigers paused beside him to scrutinize his son. The *boppeli* blinked owlishly. "We're getting ready for baby B. Are you going to be okay with him?"

"Ja," Ben breathed. "Is it all right if I step outside?"

The midwife nodded. "That's fine." Before she returned her attention to Rachel, she held Ben's gaze in a meaningful exchange. "Call me if you need anything."

Ben tried to nod, but couldn't. With his son in his arms, he stepped out of the bedroom, leaving the door ajar behind him. He was wandering about the living area, introducing his son to everything he could think of, when minutes later, there was no question that the sound now coming from the bedroom was a *hoppeli* crying. He turned to see Susannah at the bedroom door.

"You have a *dochder*, as well," she informed him, a gentle smile on her face. "She's *gut*. Healthy. Already loud, as you can hear. And no apparent jaundice on either." The last was said with a heartfelt murmur.

Ben blinked rapidly against the unexpected tears that filled his eyes. "*Gott* is *gut*. *Denki*. How's Rachel doing?" he asked hoarsely.

"She's been *wunderbar* throughout this."

Ben couldn't agree more.

"She's holding the new little *maedel*. I think she's about ready for some rest though. Do you want me to take him?" She nodded toward the bundle in his arms.

Unconsciously, Ben shifted his shoulders in protection of his son. Susannah smiled with understanding before ducking back into the bedroom.

Glancing down at the tiny figure in his arms, Ben caught his breath when he found his son looking back. He'd heard they couldn't see much at first, but still, the little one's intensity made him wonder. "Did you hear that? You have a little *schweschder*. Although I don't know how she could be littler than you." The miniature mouth opened in a yawn as the translucent eyelids drifted shut.

"That's right. Get your rest. Sounds like you're going to need it to keep up. Would you like to meet her?"

Ben returned to the bedroom. Rachel, propped up on the bed with a bundle duplicate to his in her arms, looked up. She smiled when she saw him. Her face revealed her weariness and remnants of her recent struggles, but to Ben, she'd never looked more lovely. Crossing to her, he carefully hitched a hip on the bed. Perusing his new daughter, he lowered their son so Rachel could see them side by side. Although still petite, and to his eye, even with only her face showing, beautiful like her *mamm*, it was obvious the little girl was bigger.

"You've got some catching up to do," he whispered to his son.

"Oh," Rachel sighed. "They're amazing."

Ben would've agreed, had he not been too choked up to do so.

He cleared the lump in his throat. "Have you thought of names?"

"We never talked about that, did we?"

"We didn't know who there'd be to name. We didn't know if we'd be naming a Fannie and Lavinia, or a Mervin and Iddo."

Smiling down at her new children, Rachel shook her head at his flippant choices. "Elijah and Amelia," she whispered.

Ben considered the two sleeping newborns. "Is that what you want?"

When Rachel looked up at him and nodded, he was lost in her dark brown eyes.

"Then that's who they'll be," he murmured. He straightened from the bed. "Now Eli and I will let you get some rest. We'll see you in a while."

Before he could leave the room, Mrs. Edigers stopped him, relieving him of the baby for what seemed an extended period of time as she reviewed the little one's condition. Her smile was tight as she handed the weightless bundle back. "He seems to be breathing all right, but he's so very small. Do you want to call…" She didn't finish the question but Ben knew what she was saying.

His heart clenched and his stomach twisted as he strove to find the proper response. Amish districts varied in their association with modern medicine. Theirs was slower to adapt in some areas, believing taking extraordinary medical measures to save a life conflicted with *Gott*'s will. But after an incident this past winter, when CPR administered by Hannah had saved the bishop during a heart attack and stents had put him on the road to recovery, some previous views were being reconsidered. Ben longed to do whatever was necessary to save his son, but although he'd subtly mentioned the topic around the community, no one had an answer for him on premature babies. When Mrs. Edigers simply nodded in understanding, Ben knew his confliction was evident on his face.

That's the way it continued the rest of the night. While Rachel slept, Ben sat holding his son, afraid he might never have another chance. He was shaken by the already fierce love he had for his children. Mrs. Edigers and Hannah came to check on them occasionally. Ben would sigh in relief any time Eli stretched or wiggled in his arms. When time ticked by and there was no movement, Ben would unwrap the baby to gently lay a finger on his chest and ensure by the shallow rise and fall of his tiny chest that his little one was still breathing.

Ben tipped his head to rest on the back of his chair. *Whatever happens, it's* Gott*'s will*, he reminded himself through the long hours. His mouth grew dry as he held his fragile son. Although he'd confessed privately to *Gott* and asked His forgiveness about wishing Rachel could be his wife when she had a relationship with his brother, he'd never confessed the sin to one of the district's ministers. Was it too late? Was this his punishment?

As fingers of light sifted through the window, he carefully rose from his seat, tucked an additional blanket around Eli against the coolness of the early fall morning and stepped out on the porch. Crossing to the railing, Ben turned so both of them faced the sun lifting in golden color on the eastern horizon. The calls of rousing birds, including the melancholy coo of a mourning dove, was a fitting accompaniment to the otherwise silence of the awakening morning. Lifting the bundle in his arms, Ben gently kissed the fine dark hairs on his son's miniature head.

After a few moments of quiet companionship, the squeak of the door announced they had company. Susannah stepped onto the porch. She paused a moment when she saw them before coming to join them at the rail.

At her questioning look, Ben's lips tipped in a rueful smile. "I just wanted to share a sunrise with him." With an understanding nod, Susannah stepped closer to peek into the blanketed bundle with a matching expression.

"How are Rachel and…Amelia doing?" It seemed so strange she had a name. It seemed so strange she was finally here. That they both were. He cuddled Eli more tightly. For now at least.

"They're doing well. They're both sleeping. It's been a tiring day, or should I say night, for them."

They watched as the shadows, cast by the rising sun and the big barn, shifted over the yard. When Ben cleared his throat, it seemed abnormally loud in the quiet of the morning. "I know whatever happens is *Gott*'s will. But do you think in this case His will is affected by our…actions? Do you think we're being punished for something we did?" The last was spoken with a shaky exhale.

Susannah's gaze dropped to the child in his arms. "Is that what you're worried about?"

Ben dipped his head.

"You've confessed, *ja*?" At his nod, she continued, "If you've confessed to *Gott*, He forgives." She tipped her head in the direction of the rising sun. "See the sunrise, so far to the east you'd never reach it?" Placing a gentle hand on Ben's arm, she urged him to the side of the porch where they could look behind the house where the sky was just starting to lighten over the rolling Wisconsin countryside. "See the sky to the west? Immense distance. Immeasurable. In the *Biewel*, Psalms says as far as the east is from the west." Releasing the grip on his arm, she pointed from one to the other. "That's how far *Gott* separates us from our sins." She shook her head. "You are forgiven. What *Gott* wills in this has naught to do with you."

Ben's shoulders sagged as if the barn across the yard had been lifted from them.

"And however you and Rachel came to be man and wife, I know you'll be *wunderbar* parents to my *kinner*. To both of them. His *schweschder* is sleeping in her cradle. At their size, it's big enough for two. Shall we put them in together? They've been companions for some time. Maybe the contact will do them both *gut*."

"*Ja*. We'll be right in." Ben lingered with Eli a moment longer on the porch, absorbing the awakening morning with a peace that'd been elusive earlier. Reentering the house to join Eli with his sister, Ben affirmed the important bond of siblings. He'd found peace with *Gott*. Now he needed to make peace with his *bruder* if he ever saw him again.

Chapter Fourteen

Rachel watched as Ben laid first Eli, then Amelia, into one cradle. They each had their own, but somehow she knew the twins liked to be together at times. They'd seemed to be getting bigger daily in the week since they'd been born, but they'd both fit in a single cradle for a bit yet. Eli still appeared as delicate as gossamer, but when he could stay awake long enough, she could tell that for him, he was eating like a draft horse after a day in the field. There was no sign of jaundice in either child. When she had a chance to sleep, Rachel slept easier than she had in months.

She was amazed at how adept she and Ben were getting after only a week of handling the *boppeli*, often with both little ones at a time. She was also amazed at how she could function on what little sleep she was getting since the two arrived. Her gaze followed Ben as he sank down with a tired sigh into his chair. He was something else that amazed her. Although always attentive to her personally, after the way he'd seemed detached when she was with child, he certainly wasn't disinterested now. Any time they squeaked, he was on his feet to check them or carry them to her to be fed. She didn't know what other new *daeds* did, but between him and the hired girl, other than the lack of sleep, Rachel had never felt more pampered.

They should never have wondered about Miriam. A little older than the normal hired girl for that type of situation, she was a treasure. Having been the oldest girl of a large family, she set right to work on the household tasks and helped with the babes as needed when she arrived a few days after they did. Blond and blue-eyed like her older *brieder*, she also had the cheerful attitude, along with her siblings' sense of humor that made her good company. At first, Rachel worried Miriam would think the sleeping arrangements in their household were strange for a married couple, but the young woman hadn't said a word nor raised an eyebrow when Ben and Rachel went to their separate bedrooms at night.

Rachel was the one wondering about the arrangements. Her eyes would follow her husband when he'd say a quiet good-night at the end of the evening, drop a gentle kiss on the babes' downy heads and disappear into his room.

He never kissed *her* good-night.

Picking up her sewing, Rachel pursed her lips. She was surprised at how much she wanted him to. When would he? Would he, ever? When did the thought of a simple kiss on the forehead from her husband move her more than good-night kisses with his *bruder*? Kisses that had easily faded from her memory.

Rachel wrinkled her nose at the short length of thread she had on her needle. A glance at the spool on the end table reminded her she'd emptied it of blue thread before she'd fed the *boppeli*. Knowing the two others in the room would run the errand for her if she as much as murmured a word, she silently pushed to her feet.

They both looked up when she stood, Ben from his paper, Miriam from where she was darning socks in another chair across the room.

"I need to get some more thread."

Miriam instantly set her darning aside. "I can get it for you."

"*Nee*, I think I remember where I stored an extra spool of this color. If you keep this up, you two will spoil me. At the end of your time here, I won't want to let you go because I won't remember how to take care of my own household."

With a smile, Miriam picked up the darning again. "At the end of my time here, I might not want to go, if it means I'll have to take up housekeeping for Gideon. Of course, he might not have found us a place to live by then and I may head back to Ohio."

"Depends how motivated he is." Ben's dimple was evident as he lifted *The Budget*. "When he's motivated, I've seen him act pretty quickly."

"*Ja*, as much as I don't look forward to sweeping up behind Gideon and cooking for him while I'm here, I want to intrude on Samuel and Gail even less," Miriam lamented. "Maybe I'll have a talk with Gail and see if she can make it a little less appealing for Gideon to keep staying there. But I don't know if that's possible. From the very little I've seen, she looks to be a *gut* cook and housewife."

"Can't be as *gut* as mine," Ben murmured from behind his paper.

The quiet words warmed Rachel as she went into her bedroom and headed for the nightstand. Lighting the lamp upon it, she pulled open the single drawer. She smiled when she saw the blue thread, just as she remembered. Pulling it out, she went to shut the draw. As it was sliding closed, her gaze landed on something she'd forgotten all about. She went still at the sight.

Aaron's letter.

Pulling the drawer farther open, she stared at the simple envelope. Rachel blinked as she tried to remember when it had arrived. She couldn't even remember what it said. With a lengthy inhale, she set the spool on top of the nightstand and withdrew the envelope. Darting a look toward the door to ensure no one was watching, she turned it over and pulled out the letter. She quickly scanned the few penned words.

Dear Rachel, I have been thinking of you. I didn't mean to hurt you. I do care for you. Aaron.

Her breath came faster. Not because of the message but at the possibility that her husband had seen it. Ben never used to enter her room, but since the babes were born, he'd been in and out frequently. He'd brought the babes to her when she was in bed. Would he have had any reason to open this nearby stand? He'd never said anything indicating he'd seen it. But, Rachel gnawed her bottom lip, neither had she when it arrived. Should she have told him?

To do so now might change things. Negatively. And she was…happy. Really happy. In fact, Rachel blushed, the letter crackling as she tightened her fist around it, the only thing that would make her happier would be to have a real marriage with her husband.

Was she happier than she'd have been with Aaron?

They'd had a lot of fun walking out, but when Rachel tried to visualize the day-to-day routine of marriage with her former beau, she couldn't see it working. Not like it was with Ben.

She stuffed the crumpled letter back into the envelope. With no return address, there was no way of responding to Aaron. It didn't matter. That part of her life was over. She was wife to Ben and mother to his *kinner*. A soft smile tilted her lips. There couldn't be a better husband or *daed* to the *boppeli*. Besides, she... cared for him. More than she'd ever thought she could.

Pinching the envelope between her fingers, she tore it, the sound strikingly loud in the quiet room. Rachel tore it again into quarters. Frowning at the multiple pieces, she tucked them back inside the drawer. She'd throw them away when Ben was out of the house. Closing the drawer on the shredded letter and that part of her past, she belatedly remembered to grab the thread as she blew out the lamp and headed for the door.

Rachel paused while still in the shadows of the room and peeped out at her husband. Now standing over the cradle, he was gazing down at the *boppeli*, a look of simple adoration on his face. Rachel's heart pounded as she watched. *Please,* Gott. *Help me know what to do so that someday he looks at me in the same manner.* Before she stepped through the doorway, Rachel pasted a smile on her face. They had their life now. It could be a *gut* life. The letter was in the past. As were any feelings she had for her husband's *bruder*.

Ben drew Sojourner to a halt in the growing line of black buggies parked in the pasture. He scrambled out in time to help Rachel and Miriam get down with the twins and the various desserts they'd brought to the first church Sunday since the babies were born. Being *hochmut* was wrong but Ben couldn't help thrusting his chest out a little in his *mutza* suit when all the other Amish women came bustling over to exclaim and coo over the two *boppeli*. Although it wasn't discussed when a woman was with child, it wasn't as if the community didn't know the babies were coming. Many had already seen them. It'd been a regular parade through their house with everyone visiting. *Gut* thing there were two, because they'd received more blankets of different types than it seemed the *kinder* could use in their lifetimes. The visits were *wunderbar* and most welcome. But he missed quiet evenings when, even though Miriam was there, it was like he and his wife had finally become a team.

"Oh, Ben, would you mind bringing in the church spread and bread loaves?" Rachel called over her shoulder.

When the women, all dressed similarly, left in a flock like geese lifting off a pond with about the same noise level, Ben sighed. He was cut off from his wife and family. As Rachel would sit on the side with the women while he'd be with the men, he wouldn't have minded walking beside her and his *kin* to the big barn. With another deep sigh, he retrieved two loaves of homemade bread and the church spread from the buggy. Tucking the latter under his arm, he fell into step beside Samuel and Gideon Schrock as they trailed the women.

"'Bout like driving cattle to the barn," Gideon observed.

"Careful, I think these'll do more than kick you if

you crowd them too much. Or they'll sure find a way to make you sorry you irritated them. I think cows are easier."

Ben chuckled at Samuel's comment. His previous coworker turned a jaundiced eye on him. "Sure, go ahead and laugh. I thought Malachi was bad, but you're setting an even worse standard for the rest of us, cosseting your wife the way I hear you're doing."

Recalling the rounded evidence under Gail's apron, Ben swung one of the loaves by its twist-tied wrapper, thumping Samuel on the chest with it. "Just you wait until…" His words fizzled out as he reddened slightly, embarrassed to mention the subject. He glanced at the two Schrock brothers. Although Gideon looked oblivious, Samuel wore an ear-splitting grin along with a faint blush under his black broad-brimmed hat.

"Ja," was all the usually loquacious Samuel said as they followed the chattering women.

During church, Ben's gaze kept drifting to the benches across the barn where his wife and Miriam held the *boppeli*. Things had been *gut* between him and Rachel lately. Really *gut*. Perhaps she was growing to care for him. He'd caught her looking at him when he was rocking the babes, a soft, approachable, yearning expression on her face. He'd thought he imagined it, or it was directed at the *boppeli* he held. Until he caught her sending it his way one night as he was heading for his bedroom, with no babies in the general area. Ben's pulse had galloped at the possibility the yearning expression was for him.

What might Rachel do if, when he was heading for bed, he dropped a good-night kiss on her forehead as well as the babies'? His pulse accelerated further. What would she say if they started a discussion about maybe just having…one bedroom?

Ben blinked several times at the loud voice that suddenly pierced his thoughts. Startled that someone might've caught on to what he was thinking, in church no less, he slumped on the backless bench as he realized the guest preacher was just getting fired up in his hour-long sermon. Flushing, Ben rubbed a hand over his bearded jaw, glad the covering concealed his blush at the prospect of finally perhaps being a normal husband to his wife.

His hand tightened on his chin as he considered the connection between his beard, the visiting minister and the members' meeting after church. They'd be starting the process of replacing one of the district's ministers. One had been chosen after Rachel's *daed*'s passing. Either the job had been too much for the one selected or the draw of a widow with a large farm in Jamesport, Missouri, had been too tempting. For whatever reason, the man had moved to Missouri to marry the widow, leaving the district short a minister again. One of the requirements for a man when he was baptized into the church was the willingness to serve in the lifelong role of minister if selected. It was a job few aspired to. For the first time in a selection process, Ben was eligible to be nominated to fill the role.

His hand crept up to cover his mouth as his eyes grew wide. He shifted his attention from the visiting preacher, obviously comfortable with the job, to John Stoltzfus who had preached the first sermon of the day, who obviously was not. Ben felt much more in accord with John, a *gut* man whom he and Rachel had confessed to last winter.

But if he was selected, he couldn't say no. Dropping his hand, Ben's gaze shifted around the interior of the big barn, where the members of their growing community sat on the backless benches, men on one side, women on the other. His heart pounded at the possibility of standing in front of them and speaking for even a minute without notes, much less an hour.

Certainly he loved *Gott* and wanted to serve Him, but the thought of serving in that capacity made the hands now clamped on his thighs sweat. How could he do such a thing? He couldn't even tell his wife that he loved her. Ben pressed his lips together as he recalled the story in the Old Testament. Moses had felt incapable of a job and *Gott* had used him to lead His people out of bondage in Egypt.

Surely if he was chosen, *Gott* would provide what he needed. Hadn't He already? Ben's attention rested on Rachel. *Gott* had given him Rachel. A blessing more than he could ever have hoped or imagined. She was gently rocking one of the *boppeli* in her arms. He didn't know which one for sure, but it was probably Eli because already his son was the more vocal of the two. Not crying, just letting one know he was there.

Ben slid the palms of his perspiring hands along his pants. If he could tell the whole district of his love for *Gott*, surely he could tell his wife of his love for her? The prospect made him dizzy with fear. Doing so would leave him exposed. What if she didn't feel the same? Would she pity him? Ben swallowed against the bitter taste in his mouth as his stomach churned. Better to have the whole community pity his efforts as a preacher than to have his wife pity him for declaring unrequited love. Better to be silent and appear a fool than speak and remove all doubt. But was he a fool for not telling her how he felt? For not having the courage to take the steps to make their marriage better?

He wouldn't remember the words now droned by this guest minister, but Ben remembered the ones of the speaker for the fire department training. *You can be comfortable, or you can be courageous. But never both at the same time.* At the time, Ben assumed the man was speaking of physical courage. Which for Ben was easier to address than courage of any other sort. But the man's words were fitting for other types of courage, as well.

Surprisingly, considering their tenseness at the outset of their marriage, he and Rachel had grown comfortable with each other. They were still living contentedly in the same house, unlike the young couple at their wedding who'd started out marriage in the same manner with a *boppeli* on the way. But was he still comfortable with…comfortable? Or could he summon the courage to make the marriage into what he yearned for? More than friends. True partners. There were no guarantees she'd ever feel the same way if he said the words first. But it was time to have the courage to do so.

Ben leaned forward on the hard bench as he considered his wife's down-bent head. He would do so at the next opportunity. It wouldn't be tonight. She and the babies would be tired tonight after their first public outing. But maybe tomorrow? They were making their marriage work. They'd developed a respect, a partnership with each other.

The chasm was Aaron. Ben's lips firmed in a mirth-less smile as he recalled it was the biblical Aaron who had spoken for his reluctant brother, Moses. It was time Ben spoke his heart. It'd been months since Aaron had left. Surely Rachel was over him by now?

His eyes prickled with emotion as he watched Rachel lift the bundle in her arms to kiss the *boppeli* she held. Would he have ever gotten over Rachel? Widening his eyes keep any hint of sentiment at bay, he forced himself to focus on the preacher's closing words. He didn't want to let his mind wander any more. Because he knew the answer was no. Ben just hoped Rachel's sentiment wasn't the same regarding his brother.

Chapter Fifteen

Rachel stared in shock at the man on the other side of the screen door. Under the flat-brimmed straw hat, he had her husband's dark hair and blue eyes. But no dimples were in sight. Even if the action would reveal he had them, this man was far, far from smiling.

"I'd heard I'd find you here." His gaze touched on where Eli was tucked in her arms, before shifting to Miriam who'd come up behind her carrying Amelia. His jaw clenched under the shadow of his hat. Rachel didn't know if it meant he hadn't heard about the *boppeli* as well, or that he had.

"Aaron." She couldn't say the obvious. That it was a surprise to see him. The look on her face must advise that. The look that jolted from shock to joy to yearning to—as she watched him stare at her *boppeli*— guilt.

"I thought you'd wait for me."

"I did." She had. For weeks. Watched and hoped, even prayed for his return. Rachel swallowed as she shifted uncomfortably. All the while pregnant with his *bruder*'s children.

Through the screen door, Aaron's unsmiling attention remained on the bundle in her arm. "Apparently not for very long."

His cynical words stabbed Rachel like the tines of a pitchfork. Aaron had perhaps not even cleared the county line and she'd been in his *bruder*'s arms. For comfort in her distress at her intended's departure, but still. Remorse soured her stomach. Eli started to fret. Rachel couldn't blame him. The soft cradle of her arms had stiffened into a tense, unyielding berth.

Things couldn't be changed, whether feelings had or not. She had to make Aaron understand that what'd happened with her and Ben hadn't been intentional. That she hadn't set out to betray him. That *they* hadn't set out to betray him.

"I… We …" She didn't know how to start.

"Yah, I got that part."

Aaron's set face indicated any explanation would have a difficult time finding a receptive ear. Still, Rachel had to try. She turned to see Miriam, although she'd put Amelia in her nearby cradle, was still a few steps behind her. Closing the distance between them, she gently transferred Eli to her. The young woman tenderly cuddled the baby, but Rachel could tell from Miriam's fierce expression that she'd be willing to throw the interloper off the porch should Rachel request it. And kick him down the drive, as well. Happily.

"I'm going to step outside." At Miriam's sharp look, Rachel continued, "It'll be all right. Aaron and I have a long history. Seeing each other again is a bit of a… shock to us both. I won't be far. Call if you or the *boppeli* need me."

Miriam nodded, but the protective look in her eyes told Rachel they'd be watched out the window and the hired girl wouldn't hesitate to dash out the door if needed. Warmed by the young woman's support and loyalty when she was clenching her own hands to keep them from trembling, Rachel repeated, "It'll be all right."

At least she hoped so. She turned to where Aaron remained, stone-faced, at the door. He wouldn't do anything to harm her physically. At least not the Aaron she'd once known. But his being here was an emotional calamity. Years of having been his sweetheart, of thinking he was *Gott*'s chosen one for her, tugged at dormant longings, vying against the renewed and deepened guilt that flooded her. Was he staying long? Had he come back for her? What would Ben do if he knew he was here? Trepidation regarding the Raber brothers' relationship in the short- and long-term weighed her steps as she opened the door and crossed the porch with Aaron falling in behind her.

He didn't say a word as he followed her to the self-sustaining swing Ben had built for her by the garden. She sank onto it, as, achingly aware of Aaron's presence a step behind her, she didn't know if her shaky legs could carry her any farther. The swing's chains squeaked and the wooden seat shifted under her, much like Rachel's world right now. She looked out at the mostly cleared garden. Some of the remaining vines were dead, just as her feelings for this man needed to be. She strove to prune the rustling dormant longings before they could take root.

Aaron stood stiffly beside the swing.

"How long have you been back?"

"About the length of time it took to stop at your,

well, what used to be your home, and then get here. For some foolish reason, I wanted to see you first."

Exhaling a tense sigh, Rachel tipped her head toward where an older car was parked in the driveway. "Are you staying, or returning to the *Englisch*?"

Aaron's lips twisted. "I *was* planning on staying. At least when I thought I had someone to stay for. Now, I don't know anymore."

Flinching, Rachel bowed her head. Regardless of what she felt or wanted—her sentiments were still blunted by shock—Aaron's folks would want him to stay. Aaron's *bruder* would want... What would Ben want? Either way, the thought Aaron would leave the community for good because of what they'd done was unbearable.

"We didn't intend for this to happen." Pressing her hands together on her lap, she lifted her head.

"Regardless of what you intended, it did happen. And now it can't be changed, can it?" Aaron's chest rose and fell under the force of his emotions. "I wonder, did you ever really care for me?"

Just as he said, it couldn't be changed. When Rachel couldn't do anything more than stare mutely at him with crumpled features, Aaron turned in disgust. "I think I'll go see my *bruder*." The last word was spat out like an unripe persimmon.

He stalked to the car. The engine roared to life. Rachel cringed at the spit of gravel as the vehicle spun out. When it charged down the lane, she burst into tears.

She cried enough to water the garden for a summer during a drought. She cried for Aaron. This wasn't the Aaron she'd known. She couldn't imagine being the recipient of the kind of betrayal she and Ben had inflicted on him. No wonder he was shocked and agitated.

She cried for herself. All she'd ever wanted was to be a wife to the man she loved and a *gut* mother to his children. She knew whose wife she was and would be as long as he lived, but she was so confused over whose wife she'd been meant to be. Forgotten romantic girlish feelings for Aaron seeped into the small patches of her mind that weren't absorbed with motherhood and homemaking. Patches that'd grown feelings for Ben. Could they ever regain their burgeoning happiness now that Aaron had returned?

She cried for the two brothers whom she'd unwittingly come between. She'd never forgive herself if she shattered what used to be a close relationship permanently.

Ben's fingers itched to urge Sojourner into a faster speed. He couldn't wait to get home and share his good news with Rachel. Things had been going so well for Schrock Brothers' Furniture that Malachi had given them all a raise. Ben couldn't have picked a better time to receive such news, with two new babies to support. His smile felt like it stretched from one buggy wheel to the other. Maybe they could save enough for their own farm with room for a bigger garden sooner than they'd thought. Sojy must've felt his excitement, because her gait quickened.

He blew out a breath. The raise would also be a good lead-in for other information he planned to share. That he loved her. Maybe admit he'd always loved her? *Nee*, that might be a little much. But it was time to tell her. Perhaps after supper, he could take her outside where it was private—on the opposite side of the house from the cattle, his lips twisted wryly—and tell her that he loved her. He was finally ready to say it. He hoped she was ready to hear it.

An oncoming vehicle was rapidly approaching on the narrow country road. Ben reluctantly checked Sojy as he guided her closer to the shoulder. The driver reduced his speed. At least he was courteous enough not to fly by and hog the road. Not recognizing the car, Ben idly glanced over as it passed. Sojy half reared and the buggy jolted toward the ditch at his involuntary jerk on the reins when he saw the driver.

Instantly soothing the offended horse, Ben craned his neck to look back down the road. His mouth went dry at the sight of the car's glowing brake lights. When it started to back up, he forced a hard swallow as his heart started to pound.

This wasn't a reunion to have in the middle of the road. Peering ahead, Ben saw the entrance to an alfalfa field. With tense hands, he directed Sojy to it, driving her far enough into the stubbled vegetation that the driver of the car, should he choose, could pull into the field entrance.

The driver hadn't hesitated. Ben heard the vehicle pull in behind him as he set the buggy's brake. His chest rose and fell as if he'd been the one racing down the road. As he stiffly climbed down from the seat, Ben didn't know what to expect as a greeting. A hug? A punch to the jaw? Both were abnormal to Plain folk. Amish didn't believe in overt display of affection. They didn't believe in physical violence either. But this was far from a normal situation.

There weren't many houses down this road and

therefore few reasons to be down it. As he didn't recall his brother being a close friend of Jethro, Ben knew
there was only one explanation for Aaron to have come
from that direction. He'd been to the house to see Rachel. He'd found out where she lived and he'd tracked
her down. If he'd wanted to see Ben, he would've
known to find him at work.

But he hadn't.

Crossing his arms over his chest, Ben clenched his
teeth. He didn't care to have his *bruder*, or any man,
hunting down his wife behind his back.

What'd been Rachel's response? Had she been an-
ticipating Aaron's arrival? Had there been more letters
since he'd found the one in the drawer?

Aaron was driving a car. Did that mean he didn't
plan to stay? Had he come back to get Rachel to go
with him this time?

The possibility of losing his family had Ben going
rigid as he watched his brother slowly climb out of the
car and shut the door.

"So you finally have something faster than what I
drive." Ben wanted to grab the words back as soon as
they escaped his mouth. In the vibrating silence, he'd
striven for some weak joke to break the tension. Not to
competitively increase it. But he couldn't stop himself.

It was going to be the fist to the mouth. Aaron was
capable of throwing one. Ben almost welcomed it.
Despite Aaron's flat-brimmed straw hat, perhaps he'd
been with the *Englisch* so long he'd forgotten that he
was Amish, or had been. Ben watched warily as his
older *bruder*'s hands clenched. When Aaron spoke,
Ben would've rather had the physical blow.

"I should've known you'd go after her the moment my back was turned."

Ben's mouth was dry. There was no way he was going to mention that Rachel had sought him out first.

"You shouldn't have left her without a word. She needed comfort."

Aaron's grimace migrated to a smirk. "Is that what you want to call it?"

Anger warred with guilt as both barreled through Ben. "You left all of us. You know, I've thought of you as many things throughout the years, but I never thought you were selfish. It was selfish, Aaron, to leave as you did, without telling anyone you were going. Where you were going. If you'd ever be back. Without reaching out to tell *Daed* and *Mamm* wherever you were, that you were safe. Makes me wonder why I thought so much of you when we were growing up. I should've been a better judge of character." Ben's gut twisted even as he spewed the angry words. More of them that he wanted to take back. He'd have climbed back into the buggy to stop the tirade if his knees weren't so shaky.

Aaron's face was pale under the brim of his hat. "I wondered what kind of reception I'd get. I didn't figure on red-carpet treatment, but I certainly didn't expect my own *bruder*," his lips curled at the word, "to betray me and steal my girl. Looks like the exhaust from my bus hadn't even cleared town when you two got together. Talk about being stabbed in the back. I should've shaken loose of you years ago if this is the thanks I get for letting you trail behind me."

"Well, don't worry about it now. Because—" Ben's gaze drifted behind Aaron to dwell on the car "—even if you think fit to return to the community, I'll figure out some way to steer clear of you."

"That's funny. Because I was, until I discovered what I was returning home to." Pivoting, Aaron strode to the car and jerked the door open. Sojourner flung up her head when the engine revved and dirt flew as the car wheeled out of the field road.

Ben sagged against the buggy's wheel. What had he done? What had come over him? He squeezed his eyes shut, his face contorted. Well, that was obvious. He was afraid. Afraid that somehow he'd lose what he was discovering he loved more than he could imagine. Rachel and the *boppeli*. Would they go with Aaron? He didn't think so, didn't think Rachel would agree to be shunned, which she would if she went. But even if she stayed physically, would she be emotionally distant again, realizing she'd married the wrong brother?

How would he face his parents, knowing his brother had left for reasons of his own before, but this time Ben was the one to drive him away?

Perhaps permanently.

Panting, he stayed by the wheel a moment with his hand pressed against his stomach, reluctant to clean out the buggy if he got sick while in it. When he finally climbed onto the seat, his movements were as slow and stiff as an old *grossdaddi*. He felt like he'd aged fifty years in the past fifteen minutes. Listlessly, he guided Sojy back onto the road. Where just a half mile back he'd been so excited to reach home, now he dreaded what he'd find there.

It was as he'd feared. Aaron had obviously been to the house. Rachel came out on the porch as he drove up the lane. Her face was pale and drawn, except for her eyes, which were red from an obviously long bout of tears. Ben lingered as long as possible taking care of Sojy and the other livestock. Trying to think of what to say. Determining it was better to be silent. Only a fool would bleat his love to a woman who loved another.

Rachel's eyes misted anew when he entered the house. How was he to respond to that? To a wife who wept when he walked in because he wasn't his brother coming home to her? To a wife who was trapped for a lifetime with him when she obviously wanted someone else?

Not even the presence of Miriam could keep the meal from being stilted, although the hired girl tried a few topics of conversation before surrendering to the tense silence around the table. Ben would've been surprised if any of them took a bite, only stirring their food around the plates. He didn't linger after supper, heading straight to his room, a solitary room that would now be endlessly his.

Chapter Sixteen

The ticking of the clock outside his bedroom marked the seconds, minutes and hours that crept by. Sleep was impossible. Ben's heart was still hammering, his stomach still churning from his conversation with Aaron and the lack of a needed one with Rachel. The only moments that'd brought peace were the ones when he held the *boppeli*. Obviously alert to his tension, they'd initially squirmed, their blue eyes seeking his face. As they'd relaxed, he had as well, the rigidity seeping from him as they eventually fell asleep in his arms.

Thinking of them, he alerted to the occasional squeaks he knew were coming from the cradles now in Rachel's room. The babies were waking. Knowing he wouldn't be sleeping, and needing their comfort again, he slipped from bed and quietly dressed. After lighting a lamp by his cushion chair, he tiptoed into Rachel's room and headed for the cradles while casting a glance toward her motionless figure on the bed.

The babies were stirring, but their *mamm* was not. Not surprising, when he'd heard her up with them two hours earlier. Although she had Miriam to help car for the house and *boppeli*, the two little ones required a lot of work. The amount of tears Rachel had obviously cried today would've also physically exhausted her. Ben quietly and carefully scooped up Amelia and Eli and carried them out of the room.

No stranger to diaper duties, he had the twins changed before they became fully awake. Glad they kept formula on hand for such occasions, Ben prepared a bottle for each and with some negotiating, settled down to feed them. It took a bit of coaxing, as the twins preferred their *mamm*, but as they grew hungrier, they latched on to the bottles.

While watching them eat, Ben again felt his tension ebb as his heart filled.

"You two will have a bond that can never be parted." Ben sighed. "You'll play together. You'll work together. You'll learn from each other. You'll probably argue at times. I imagine Eli will tug on your hair, Amelia, if it's not the other way around." The backs of Ben's eyes prickled at the thought of the two wee ones in his arms having discord in their lives that couldn't be repaired. The possibility broke his heart.

"But you'll love each other. You'll learn and understand the other's strengths and weaknesses. We all have weaknesses." Ben bit his lip as he gazed at his children, who studied him solemnly in return. "You need to stand up for each other. You're family."

Their little faces grew blurry as Ben blinked back tears. He couldn't leave things this way with Aaron. Pride and fear shouldn't get between family. Closing his eyes, he grimaced as his awful words this afternoon echoed in his head. If he had driven Aaron away, Ben didn't know how he'd forgive himself.

When he opened his eyes, he found the babies regarding him with concern. Their mirrored expressions raised a misty smile. "Being silent in this case would be more than appearing a fool. It would mean being one. I need to go talk to him, don't I? Apologize. For a lot of things. Should I tell him I always l—" Ben had to clear his throat to get the word out. "Always loved your *mamm*? I suppose that's something a child wants to hear. Or at least know that their *daed* loves their *mamm*. It's something she probably wants to know, as well. But I don't know if I can tell her, now that the man she really loves is back. See, we can't change things, but I don't want to rush her, like I feel I did to…" Ben smiled "…have the surprise of your arrival. I want to give her time. I wouldn't feel right to be a couple when she's thinking of someone else."

Amelia's little brows furrowed as she sucked at the bottle harder.

"*Ach*, please don't think me a coward for not telling her. It's enough that you two know now. By the time you can tell her, maybe we'll have worked something out. In the meantime, just know that I'm here for you and her, and I cherish all three of you more than you can ever imagine."

Eli's eyelids were getting heavy. Ben jiggled him gently to wake him enough to eat a bit more. "Anyway, regarding Aaron, I feel I cheated my *bruder*. Always wanted and then had a chance to take something that was his. I can see why he feels upset and betrayed. This life with your *mamm* should've been his. You should've been his." Ben's arms tightened around the babes. "But I thank *Gott* every day that you're mine. Already I can't imagine living without you."

Removing the finished bottles and shifting Eli to his lap, he lifted Amelia to his shoulder to gently coax a burp. "But I can't imagine existing with this discord between Aaron and me. I must apologize. I hope he'll forgive me." Achieving success with Amelia, he switched the babes' positions. "Even if he doesn't, at least I'll know I've tried to set things right."

Balancing both *boppeli* on his lap, he watched their eyes drift shut as he carefully swaddled them. "Thanks for the talk. You're both *gut* listeners. I'll talk to Aaron as soon as possible. With your *mamm*, we'll give her some more time. I'm trusting you two to keep what I said a secret." He rose from his chair. Bending first one arm, then the other, he kissed both their brows and quietly slipped into his sleeping wife's bedroom to return his children to their cradles.

Ben left the farm following chores early the next morning, glad it was a Saturday and he could put the onerous task behind him. With a parting glance at the house, his lips twitched, knowing the babes wouldn't tell Rachel that it was he, and not Miriam, who'd got ten up with them in the middle of the night. Knowing they wouldn't share his other admissions either. His smile faded as he turned Sojy at the end of the lane. Now he had to keep his vow. He was guessing Aaron, if he hadn't already departed again, would be staying at their folks' farm. If not, maybe his *daed* would know where to find him. Even though he dreaded doing so.

Several pensive miles later, Ben sighed in relief at the sight of yesterday's car parked in front of his family farm's big white barn. His chest tightened when Aaron came to the barn door, a pitchfork in his hand, as Ben drew Sojy to a stop next to the vehicle. The two brothers watched each other warily as Ben set the brake and stepped down from the buggy.

When his feet hit the ground, Ben remained rooted for a moment. "Where's *Daed*?" It seemed a safe place to start. He hadn't decided if he wanted a witness to what he needed to say.

"He and *Mamm* went into town." Aaron gave a studiously negligent shrug. "They said they had errands, but I imagine they wanted to share the news about the prodigal son returning."

Glancing over at the car, Ben shifted his feet. "And has he?"

The admission was slow in coming. "Probably."

"Where's the rest of the family?" Ben tried to peer into the quiet depths of the barn. "Our two younger *brieder* aren't helping you?"

"I told them I had it. After being stared at, tiptoed around and asked how I was doing for the past sixteen hours, I was ready for a little alone time."

"I guess that's something I didn't ask yesterday." Needing something to do with his hands, Ben scratched the back of his neck. "How *are* you doing?"

"I've been better."

Ben nodded toward the shadowy barn behind Aaron's stiff figure. "You still want alone time, or do you want some help?"

"I remember how to muck a stall, if that's what you're asking."

"I learned how to muck out one pretty well too, because someone did a *gut* job of teaching me."

For the first time, a shadow of a smile touched

Aaron's face. "He should've taught you to respect your elders."

Ben was surprised he didn't collapse to the ground in a heap with the relief that swept through him. "You're not that much older."

"Old enough that you're still an irritating little *bruder.*" Aaron gestured with his head. "Come on. There's work enough for two. Or maybe I'll just let you take over. You seem to be *gut* at that."

Already moving toward the barn door, Ben hesitated at his words. Aaron's face was now in the barn's shadows. He couldn't see his *bruder*'s expression. With a heavy thickness in his throat, he stepped into the barn. Following Aaron to the wooden wall where various tools hung by hooks and nails, he removed a pitchfork.

"About…that." Resting the pitchfork on the ground, tines down, Ben curled his hands around the wooden handle. "I'm sorry for what I said yesterday. I'm sorry for a lot of things. I can't imagine what you must have felt coming back to find…the situation you did." Ben blew out a breath through pursed lips. When Aaron didn't respond, only met his eyes with a steady gaze and set expression, Ben continued, "I want you to know that none of this was Rachel's fault. We didn't mean for what happened…to happen. We were both upset when you left. I let things go too far. Then when she told me—" he swallowed hard "—about the *boppeli,* and we didn't know if or when you were coming back, we had to do something."

Still no reaction from his *bruder.* Looking away from the man's obviously clenched jaw, Ben shifted his attention to the line of stalls on the far side of the barn, where the brown heads of his *daed*'s Standardbreds were watching them curiously. "It wouldn't have mattered, but for a while I wondered if it was…"

"We never did that. Rachel and I. Don't think that of her."

Ben reluctantly returned his gaze to Aaron. "*Ja*, I know that now."

Aaron pivoted to stride a few steps and stab the pitchfork into a bale of straw lying in front of an empty stall. Dust and small bits of yellow chaff flew into the air and Ben tightened his hands on his own pitchfork handle when Aaron unexpectedly kicked the bale. He blinked in surprise when his *bruder* heaved a heavy sigh and turned to sink down upon it.

"That was part of the problem."

"What?" Ben cocked his head at the unexpected response.

"I didn't ever think of her…that way." Aaron rested his chin on fisted hands propped up by his elbows on his knees. "Rachel is a *wunderbar* girl. Fun. An easy companion. I don't think there's a better girl in the district. But as time went, I began to think of her more as a *schweschder* than a girlfriend. I still love her… but not in that way. Surely there's something more in a married relationship than that?" He regarded Ben as if his *bruder* might have an answer.

Ben thought of how much he loved his wife. Deeply, in so many ways, but none of them sisterly. Aaron was right to wonder.

"I didn't know what to do. Everyone had expectations for us. Her *mamm*. Our parents. The whole community. The thought of marrying her and having her as a wife forever…" He shook his head. "But I didn't want to hurt her, or embarrass her publicly by breaking up right before everyone expected a wedding."

"Disappearing instead wasn't a promising alternative." Ben's jaw tightened as he recalled the pain Rachel went through.

Aaron ducked his head. "I know. I was a coward. I don't care for conflict or the thought of hurting someone. It's pretty sad when you're glad to be kicked by a horse. Probably too bad I didn't get kicked in the head. I was relieved when I broke my arm and my baptism was delayed. There was so much pressure to be baptized and then married. I still wasn't sure what I wanted. And even if we did marry, I needed a way to support her. But I hurt her anyway. I hurt both of you." His gaze met Ben's wide eyes. "For that I'm sorry."

Ben didn't know if he'd be able to stay upright without the support of the pitchfork.

Aaron snorted. "I actually came back to be baptized. Marry Rachel. Here I came to be noble and go through with it all. You wouldn't even let me do that. Just like things got before I'd left, you'd already done it for me. I think that's what upset me so. The shock of how things had changed and all the self-debating I went through before finally determining to do the honorable thing and live up to everyone's expectations." Pushing to his feet, he stepped toward Ben.

"Do you still love her?" Ben watched his *bruder* approach. The answer made all the difference, but he couldn't make the question more than a whisper.

"*Ja*. But not in the way you do." Aaron clamped his hand on Ben's shoulder. "Maybe it was prophetic of me to think of her as a sister, because that's what she is now. My sister-in-law."

"I couldn't leave things the way they ended yesterday. Our relationship means too much to me."

Aaron squeezed his shoulder. "Me too."

"I'm afraid she still loves you."

Aaron winced. "We'll work around that."

Tension seeped from Ben. With Aaron willingly yielding the field, somehow, someway, he and Rachel would work it out. He couldn't suppress the silly grin that slipped onto his face. "Maybe she just needs to get to know you better. You'd only shown her your charming side. And I know from experience, it's very limited."

Aaron released Ben's shoulder with a brotherly shove. Ben didn't budge. "Why waste charm on a little *bruder*? They're stuck with you anyway." His eyes narrowed on Ben as he smiled crookedly. "Maybe along with mucking out a stall, I should've coached you on how to be charming to women. But, as you've somehow managed to be married anyway, I guess I'll have to take my charm and find another woman to practice it on."

"You won't find a better one."

"I can tell you believe that. I'm glad for you." Aaron observed Ben solemnly. "I'm glad for Rachel, as well. Loving her like a sister, I want the best for her. And I know she won't find a better man than the one she has."

Ben glanced away. He couldn't respond for the lump in his throat. When he looked back to his brother, Aaron was smiling ruefully.

Aaron sighed exaggeratingly. "I guess, since I'm back, hopefully there's someone worthy out there I can scare up." Aaron turned to jerk the pitchfork from the straw bale. "In the meantime, I'll show you that, even though it's been awhile, I can still outwork my little *bruder*."

"I don't know." Shifting his pitchfork to one hand, Ben strode over to a half-filled wheelbarrow. "I had a *gut* teacher."

"I don't suppose you need a car," Aaron mused as he entered the empty stall behind him.

"No more than you do," Ben replied, pushing the wheelbarrow within his *bruder*'s reach.

"Maybe I can find some young fool entering his *rumspringa*. They think they know everything then."

The two brothers set to work. Ben didn't know what Aaron's thoughts were, but his, now that he'd worked up the courage to resolve the relationship from his past, were on how to bolster his courage even more to resolve the vital one of his future.

Chapter Seventeen

Only exhaustion had freed Rachel from her thoughts and allowed her to sleep last night. When Ben didn't come in after chores, her anxiety, already high, ratcheted up another degree. She wanted to talk with him. She *needed* to talk with him. She'd intended to this morning, but he'd left instead—to where, she didn't know. By the time his rig finally pulled into the lane later in the morning, she'd almost worn a path in linoleum pacing to the window. Aaron's return had fractured the relationship she and Ben had worked so hard to create. Would they be able to mend it again?

Her heart thudded when Ben stepped into the kitchen. Its cadence, which marginally calmed when his gaze—touching first on her, then on Amelia in her arms—accelerated again when a smile tipped his lips. Relieved, confused, Rachel could do no more than return a mute stare.

In the silence that pulsed throughout the tidy room, Ben finally spoke. "I saw Isaiah Zook this morning. He's planning to move some more steers over here. I need to finally get that bunk fixed."

Rachel rested a hip against the counter. Was he expecting her to balk at the news? It wasn't the conversation she wanted, needed, but after yesterday, at least they were talking. But this was Ben's choice of topic after that emotional upheaval? She glanced at the nearby open door, where Miriam was currently emptying the manual washing machine. The conversation she wanted didn't need an audience, even a sympathetic one. She'd have to find a more solitary time and place to initiate it.

At her hesitant nod, Ben continued, "I'll be working on it for the rest of the morning. Call me when lunch is ready?"

Once more, Rachel nodded. Ben opened his mouth to speak, only to close it when his gaze also lit on where Miriam was visible doing laundry. But his hesitant smile lifted even more, until there was a slight promise that the dimple Rachel had grown to treasure might put in an appearance. What did it mean? She was left to wonder as he turned and went out the door.

And wonder she did. Through feeding the twins and putting them in their cradles. Through preparing a casserole while Miriam took the laundry to hang on the clothesline. Through washing up utensils. While doing so, Rachel glanced out the kitchen window at the loud rattle being generated from the farmyard. Ben had emptied the pen in order to work. The steers, now shut in the pasture along with Billy and the other bulls, were roughhousing with each other. Some were knocked against the metal gate that kept them from the pen where Ben was repairing the feed bunk. She furrowed her brow as the gate lifted upon the pressure of one of the many broad black-and-white heads that crowded against it. The rusty gate dropped back down with a squeak, followed by a bang.

Frowning, Rachel's attention moved from the cattle to the man currently sawing a board at the opposite side of the bare dirt pen. She envied him the physical task, knowing busy hands calmed the mind. She'd known he'd wanted to fix it for a while, but events—his injury, the arrival of the *boppeli*—*had* forestalled it. Maybe the bunk needed mending right at this moment. Or maybe it was just an excuse to get out of the house. And away from her and a needed conversation?

But that's not what his parting smile had said. Although not actually speaking, Rachel snorted—that was Ben's way—his smile had said…hope. Hope for them to find a way through the shock of Aaron's return? Hope and a way the three of them could reside harmoniously together going forward in the community?

Rachel knew her heartache of yesterday wasn't because she wanted to be with Aaron. *Ja*, she cared for him and hoped that he could find happiness somehow. But she'd realized her shock and grief at his return had been for the impact to her and Ben's growing relationship. She'd become…happy with Ben. Very happy. The thought of continuing to build a life with him and their children made her want to crow like an overzealous rooster.

Did he have any inkling of how she felt? Rachel's fingers clenched on the sink as Ben paused sawing for a lingering look toward the house. She'd been one who'd needed to be told she was appreciated in order to feel worthy. Just because Ben wasn't one for saying the words didn't mean he never wanted to hear them.

Did he know her feelings for Aaron had faded away? That it'd been an annual blooming in its time and not a perennial that would grow stronger every year, like her feelings for Ben?

How could he know, if she hadn't told him?

Rachel discarded the possibility of talking to him in the evening. By the time the *boppeli* were put to bed—with the knowledge they would wake again in a few hours—both she and Ben would be tired. Too tired for this type of discussion. Besides, he didn't seem to welcome deep conversations. Facing a reluctant communicator in a quiet room with only the ticking of the wall clock could get awkward. Much better to talk with him when his hands were busy and there were other distractions. And if the conversation didn't go well— Rachel drew in a shaky breath at the possibility—it would be easier to be outside and return to the house on some premise than have the discussion later that night and need to retreat silently to her bedroom after a stilted talk.

Scanning the kitchen, she looked for some excuse to go outside. As Miriam stepped back inside with an empty laundry basket, Rachel's gaze landed on a pitcher drying on the dish rack.

"I'm taking a glass of lemonade out to Ben. I'll be back shortly. Call me if the twins wake up." Snagging the pitcher and hastily making the lemonade, Rachel poured a glass and headed for the door.

Crossing the porch, she steadied herself with a few deep breaths. She was going to tell her husband she cared for him. Surely brides did that all the time. Although most do it before they're married. And probably definitely before they have two children. Rachel grimaced as lemonade sloshed out of the glass over her trembling hand. At this rate, she'd be fortunate to have anything in the glass by the time she reached him. Focusing on Ben, bent over the end of the bunk as he hammered in a board, she started across the driveway, the gravel barely noticeable under the summer-toughened soles of her feet.

In the months they'd lived there, she'd never been all the way across the gravel to the strip of grass along the pen fence. Except for when Ben, severely injured, had been lying under the bunk. She was relieved that now, like then, the lot was empty. Otherwise, she didn't know if she'd be able to get close enough to hand Ben the glass, much less stay and talk.

How should she start this vital conversation? Rachel searched for words to say after *would you like some lemonade?* Should she make small talk? Ask about the cattle, as they were right there in their domain? Her lips twitched. That'd surprise Ben and throw him off balance. Maybe that's what he needed. Also, it would show him she was interested in what he was interested in. Hopefully easing from that into what she was interested in. Whom she cared for. Whom she loved.

Looking toward the pasture gate to get some conversation inspiration from the black-and-white beasts, Rachel stumbled to a halt, sloshing lemonade. While the other cattle had drifted away from the gate to graze in the pasture, over the top white rails she could see the big black back of the bull, Billy. She'd grown used to seeing him standing by the secured gate, broodingly watching the steers when they were in the pen. But something was wrong. Was he in the pasture or in the pen? For a moment, she couldn't tell. Her frantic gaze finally located the gate, sagging low to the ground next to the deserted post used to secure it.

Billy was loose in the pen.

His attention was fixed on Ben, still bent over his task and unaware of the present danger. The mostly black head was lowered and visible between the white rails. Chills ran up Rachel's spine at the bull's large, protruding eyes. As he pawed the bare dirt, clods of it flew up to dust the black sleekness of his arched back.

Her gaze darted back to her unsuspecting husband. Rachel opened her mouth to scream. To her horror, no sound resonated in warning. Her breath was locked in her chest. Her feet frozen on the gravel of the driveway. As she watched the bull's stealthy progress across the pen, unbidden, a thought prickled into her mind.

A widow would be free to marry again.

And no one would be surprised to see a man marry his deceased *bruder*'s young widow and take responsibility for his *kinder*.

Rachel clenched her hand, the ridged design of the glass cutting into her white-knuckled fingers. For a moment, she stared at it blankly. A second later, lemonade splashed over the gravel as her arm cocked. Breaking free of her rigid stupor, she lunged forward. Finding her voice, Rachel yelled at the top of her lungs. Still a few feet from the fence, she launched the glass into the pen. It fell beside one large cloven hoof. The bull didn't turn his broad head.

But when Rachel smacked into the fence and scrambled up it, she had his attention. Climbing up until the top rail pressed against her hips, Rachel leaned over it, waving her hands above her head while shrieking for all she was worth. Billy spun to face this new challenge. As Rachel sucked in a breath for another scream, her heart stuttered at the bull's rumbling huffs. She couldn't risk a glance away to confirm Ben had been alerted to the danger.

With a mighty bellow, Billy charged.

Rachel's piercing scream was squelched when hands grabbed about her waist and jerked her backward off the rails. Breathless from surprise and the tumble to the ground, she flinched when the fence cracked as Billy hit it. The post leaned, but held. Dirt flew as the bull nimbly spun to peer through the rails with his bulging eyes. Rachel's heartbeat hammered in her ears as he banged his head against what now seemed a flimsy barrier. With a final snort, Billy pivoted and arrogantly trotted away.

All the energy vaporized from Rachel. Her head flopped back against the moving pillow that cradled it.

"Are you all right?" The question rumbled as much from Ben's chest beneath her ear as from his frantic tone behind her head.

For a moment, Rachel's rapid panting prevented an answer. She realized, as her head was bobbing up and down in its position on Ben, he was breathing briskly, as well. Knowing her head was nodding in an accidental affirmation to his question struck her as funny. Was this shock? She began to giggle. Feeling his racing heartbeat under her ear and knowing he was safely there with her, that the bull hadn't hurt him, overwhelmed her with emotion. A few sobs joined the giggles until she was crying in earnest.

Twisting, she pressed her cheek against his chest, curling her fingers into his shirt as she wet it with her tears. Carefully holding her, Ben struggled to sit up. "Rachel! Rachel! Did he hurt you?"

Shaking her head, she sniffed loudly. *"Nee,"* she confirmed nasally.

"What is it then?" Urgent concern punctuated his words.

"I'm just so glad he didn't hurt you." She continued to shake her head. "I don't know what I'd do without you. I love you so much."

Ben's heart rate under her car picked up even as he went motionless. Rachel stilled, as well. Drawing a few shuddering breaths, she lifted her gaze to meet his stunned blue eyes. Dazedly shifting into a seated position on the grass, he pulled Rachel into his lap, positioning her so they still faced each other.

"When? How?" His face tightened fractionally. "Is it because of the *boppeli*?"

"Ja," she admitted. "It's because of the *boppeli*."

The dismay on his face would've been imperceptive, except that she knew it so well. Lifting her hand, she laid it against his cheek. "If it weren't for the *boppeli*, I might've missed you. And I can't bear the thought of that."

Ben's eyes glowed. Turning his head slightly, he kissed the palm of her hand.

Miriam came out on the porch. With a concerned frown at the sight of them on the ground, she hastened down the steps. "Is everything all right?"

Glancing at each other, they grinned. Rachel felt his dimple crease under her hand. She'd been scrutinizing the *boppeli*, hoping at least one might have their *daed*'s dimples. *"Ja.* Everything is all right. Everything is really *gut*, in fact."

Regarding them oddly, Miriam shook her head and returned to the house.

Rachel brought her hand down. "She probably thinks we're nuts."

"We are. Or at least I am. I'm nuts about you. And maybe both of us together. We didn't go about this marriage in the normal way. *Boppeli* first, then marriage. Followed lastly by a clumsy courtship." Ben cradled her in his arms. Rachel felt his kiss against her hair. "Any regrets about the way things worked out?"

Did she? Knowing now how it ended. How it always should've ended. How she was so very, very glad it ended. Safe, secure, thrilled to be in his arms, she nodded. "*Ja*. One."

She felt his indrawn sigh surround her as he prepared himself for her response. Dear, quiet, always supportive Ben, whose expressions weren't always verbal, but were strongly communicated nonetheless. "What is it?"

"That I didn't walk out with you first and only."

Ben kissed her. For their first, it was one worth waiting for. And, as Rachel melted into his arms, she definitely knew it wouldn't be their only.

Moments later, Ben rested his cheek against hers. "That's *gut*," he murmured. "Because for me, it's always been you. And only you."

Epilogue

"Are you sure she doesn't mind?" Rachel was glad her voice didn't reflect her jitters.

Ben's hand was a reassuring presence on her elbow. Even though she didn't turn, she knew his dimples were in appearance. "I'm sure. The cows aren't just standing outside the barn door at night because they want some food. By that time of day, they want to be milked."

Rachel flushed, recalling how she felt when the twins hadn't nursed in a while. Tentatively, she reached toward the large black-and-white figure a short arm's length away and drew in a shuddering breath. Touching the cow with trembling fingers, Rachel squeaked and jumped back when the skin tightened and lifted beneath her hand. Ben's hand at her waist steadied her, but she could hear his chuckle over the cow's ensuing *moo* that echoed through the Lapps' milking parlor.

Maybe it was his presence in her life that steadied her. She couldn't imagine hers without it. Or without month-old Eli and Amelia, currently inside the Lapps' house, being doted upon by *grossmammi* Susannah and Gail and Hannah's mother, Willa Lapp, while she and

Ben were in the barn, borrowing the dairy farmer's most gentle cow to help Rachel face her fear.

She was so glad the bull, Billy, was gone. Isaiah had sold him quickly after the last incident, proclaiming he'd rather have his friends alive than the best milking herd in the county.

"It's okay. Blossom is just asking where the rest of the girls are. She's not used to having the place to herself." Taking Rachel's hand under his own, he gently placed it against the cow's side again. Rachel's fingers curled slightly into the warm hide, marveling at the live tension pulsing under her palm in the Holstein's large belly.

"Are you sure you want to try to milk her today, or are you *gut* and is this enough for now?"

Rachel smiled at his words. Her apprehensive body's rigidity evaporated as she leaned back against his sturdy chest. This was enough. Ben was enough. He was much, much more than enough. For now and always. Rotating her hand, she braided her fingers with his. His arms tightened around her as he rested his chin against her hair.

While *Gott* had always known Ben was her chosen one, she'd had more of a journey to make the discovery. Lifting their entwined grasp from the cow's side, Rachel pressed the back of his hand against her cheek. How could she not have seen before that he was the one? It was right there in front of her in, well, black-and-white.

Whatever her fears, now and in the future, she knew she could face them with this man by her side.

She closed her eyes with a heartfelt sigh. "*Ja.* I'm *gut.* I'm very, very *gut.*"

* * * * *

If you loved this story,
check out these other Amish romances
by Jocelyn McClay

The Amish Bachelor's Choice
Amish Reckoning
Her Forbidden Amish Love

Available now from Love Inspired!

Find more great reads at www.LoveInspired.com

Dear Reader,

Thanks for joining me at Miller's Creek, whether you're returning or arriving for the first time!

Fifteen years into my marriage, my uncle mentioned a book on love languages. Reading it opened my eyes to the realization that my husband and I communicated our love in totally different ways. I'd expected him to express his affection in the way I interpreted love, while he'd been conveying it in the way he understood. It wasn't until I understood his method that I realized and appreciated how loudly he'd been speaking it.

Rachel and Ben are in the same situation. He doesn't express his love in the manner she understands, but he revealed it instead in his own quiet way.

Ben's way doesn't include verbally opening his heart. While researching for the story, I learned that courage originally meant expressing one's heart. Expressing one's heart can make us vulnerable, which is something even heroes—though they're willing to face other risks—might struggle to find the bravery to do.

Thanks again for visiting the Miller's Creek community! Several readers have asked for Jethro's story. Rest assured, he'll find his happily-ever-after in the next Miller's Creek story (can you guess who his heroine will be?). In the meantime, you can find me on Facebook or at jocelynmcclay.com.

May God bless you,
Jocelyn McClay

**WE HOPE YOU ENJOYED
THIS BOOK FROM**

LOVE INSPIRED

INSPIRATIONAL ROMANCE

Uplifting stories of faith, forgiveness and hope.

Fall in love with stories where faith helps
guide you through life's challenges, and discover
the promise of a new beginning.

6 NEW BOOKS AVAILABLE EVERY MONTH!